STRIKE OF DEATH

The Night Ghost stood with his legs braced apart, right leg straight, knee of the left leg slightly bent, most of his weight on the forward right leg. His hands were clenched into double fists, the right drawn in close to his chest, his left fully extended—his openly hostile attitude and overall stance branding him to Frost as a practitioner of hard-style kung fu.

Shifting suddenly on his feet the Night Ghost attacked, leaping forward out of his basic front stance, right fist driving out in a thumb-knuckle strike for his opponent's solar plexus. But the blow never landed, was retaliated with a perfectly timed palm-heel block, flying in front of his body, deflecting the Night Ghost's punch out and away, then quickly following up the block with a well-executed palm-heel strike that struck the stunned Night Ghost hard in the face.

The black-clad fanatic stumbled back in surprise, made a growling noise deep in his throat, and attacked again. . . .

#16

THEY CALL ME

THE

MERCENARY

CHINA BLOODHUNT

BY AXEL KILGORE

ZEBRA BOOKS
KENSINGTON PUBLISHING CORP.

ZEBRA BOOKS

are published by

KENSINGTON PUBLISHING CORP.
475 Park Avenue South
New York, N.Y. 10016

First printing: November, 1983

Printed in the United States of America

For Walter, Roberta, Leslie, Michael, and Liselle—
all with much patience and good will, who have
helped the one-eyed man keep fighting.

Chapter One

Hong Kong translated to the Place of Sweet Lagoons, at least as far as all the travel brochures were concerned, but to Hank Frost, walking late at night alongside the docks adjacent to Victoria Harbor, the setting had all the earmarks of a trap—the kind where it's grease and silk getting in, blood and nails getting out.

The one-eyed man, nervous in the unfamiliar surroundings, reached into the right outside pocket of his jacket, finding the rumpled pack of Camels, fumbling one of them out. He found his lighter, flicking back the cowling, rolling the striking wheel under his thumb, then fed the tip of the cigarette into the battered Zippo's blue-yellow flame. He popped the lighter closed with a soft metallic click, then dropped it into a pocket. He inhaled, taking the smoke deep into his lungs, mentally sizing up the situation at hand. From the moment he and O'Hara had entered the dock area Frost had smelled more than garbage and sea water—there was going to be trouble. "Damn," he muttered.

"You can say that again, sport," O'Hara snarled. "This whole deal's sucked right from the beginning. What in the hell are we doing down here at this time of night, anyway? I tell ya, Frost, without my .44, I feel naked."

"Yeah." Frost mentally and physically shrugged, then kept walking, moving faster now, his tall, lanky friend from the FBI matching the increased tempo of his pace, step for step. The one-eyed man cocked his ear to the right, listening intently to the diverse sounds of water traffic traversing the harbor, wishing to himself that the thick fog hadn't blanketed the docks twenty minutes earlier, obscuring everything farther out than three feet away in its swirling curtain of dense, damp gray. "If we were to go barging down the street like we owned the city or something, all we'd likely do is to scare off our contact and then we could forget about getting whatever information it is he's supposed to have for us."

"And I don't like that part one bit, neither," O'Hara barked, Frost deciding that, while his older friend might have been in one of his ripe moods for complaining, the FBI agent was still batting a thousand in the logic department. What did they know about the real reason behind their visit to Hong Kong? Not enough to fill a post card. All they had been told was to come to the dock area at a specified time, go for a walk like they did it every night of the week, and then wait for their contact—they didn't even know his name or what he looked like—to make himself known. It was all very cut and dry, but it was, Frost knew, the very simplicity of the operation that could back them into a corner.

The one-eyed man felt O'Hara nudge him gently in the side. "What's the time, Ace?"

"Five minutes later than the last time you asked," Frost confirmed, glancing through the increasingly heavy fog at the black-faced Rolex Sea-Dweller on his left wrist. It was 10:37. Their contact was already a half hour late—that fact in itself tempting Frost to call the whole clandestine meeting off, and to respond to the crawly feeling at the edge of his senses by getting himself and O'Hara as far away from the docks as possible. A no-show like this usually meant trouble.*

*See THEY CALL ME MERCENARY #12, Headshot

8

"We'll give it five minutes more," Frost said, not expecting any objections from O'Hara. "After that we double back the way we came and head for the hotel."

"Awww, another five minutes won't make any difference, Frost. Face it, the boys in the State Department screwed up—they shoulda known better than to expect some lousy Commie son-of-a—"

"Hold it, Mike." When they had first started their walk the occasional passerby had been limited to various dock workers involved in transporting goods from one point to another, a couple of sailors, Frost remembered, who had been speaking German, plus a solitary bicycle rider who had nearly collided with a startled O'Hara's rear end—after that, no one.

For the last half mile their only company had been the growing mists of fog and each other. But now, Frost squinting to make sure his eye wasn't playing tricks on him, they were no longer alone. Up ahead, the exact distance difficult to judge due to the fog, silhouetted beneath the halo of a yellowish, flickering street lamp, stood a lone figure, back pressed against the wall of some kind of specialty shop, right foot off the ground resting upon what appeared to be a short stack of bricks.

"Could be our contact, O'Hara. Whatta ya say?"

O'Hara, shrugging noticeably as they kept walking, spoke quickly out of the side of his mouth. "If it is our contact, I'm gonna ask him why the hell he was so late."

"If he's our man, you be my guest. If he's not . . ." Frost let the statement hang, unfinished, as the figure—it was definitely a man—waiting beneath the street light, turned at the sound of their approach, a wide smile spreading instantly across his face.

"Good evening, gentlemen," the Chinese spoke first, his English smooth and confident, his smile even wider—exhibiting all the genuine warmth of a painted piece of cardboard, Frost thought. "Where have you

9

been all my life?"

"Where have we been?" O'Hara jumped in, pointing an accusing finger at the placid Chinese. "You know where we've been—walking up and down these damn docks here, lookin' for you."

"And most gracious of you to do so, sir. You are American, correct?"

"Both of us," Frost cut in, "right down to the part about mom and apple pie. Now, do you have something for us, or not?"

"Oh, no, quite the opposite. It is you who have something for me."

The one-eyed man man looked to his friend. "Uh oh, I don't think this is our contact."

"No shit."

Then the Chinese casually placed the first two fingers of his right hand to his lips and blew, letting loose with a shrill four note whistle, obviously a signal of some sort. Immediately, it seemed, faces and bodies appeared out of the fog, out of nowhere, close to a dozen in all, bunching together in a tight ring around Frost and O'Hara, each newcomer wielding a weapon.

"I'm afraid you're at a disadvantage," Frost told the first man, the apparent ringleader of the gang, bringing a reflection of the man's arrogant smile to his own face. Surrounded as they were within a tightening circle of knives, chains, and steel pipes—the ringleader had one of those—a wrong move at this stage could spell disaster. "There are twelve of you, two of us. You guys might be in trouble. So what's the story, huh? Who the hell are you, anyway?"

"Hey, you gotta be kidding me, American with the one eye," the ringleader shot back, almost sounding offended. "Everybody know who we are! We the Fat Cats—Number One teddy boy gang in all of Hong Kong! We rob from the rich and give to the poor, only

10

in this case, we the poor we give it to." And at that he laughed out loud, much louder and harder than necessary, the rest of his followers joining in.

"Don't get me wrong," Frost explained as the forced laughter began to die down. "I like the poor just as much as the next guy, but the thing is, ahh, you and your . . . ?"

"Fat Cats!"

"Fat Cats, right, yeah . . . well, you and your Fat Cats just made a big mistake. My tall friend and I may look like rich Americans see, but we're not. Tell you the truth," and Frost gestured conspiratorially with his left index finger to where his missing eye was covered, "see—this is the only eye patch I own. I have to wash it out and dry it every night before I go to bed."

The ringleader smirked. "That too bad for you. It also too bad for you if you and your friend don't empty your pockets now and give everything to us. We in a hurry, very late now. Must get home to our families. You do like I say and no one get hurt. We be generous—you do like I say, we let you keep your clothes. Okay, American?"

Frost let his shoulders sag. "You want our money?"

"That's right, American—we want your money!" He gestured with the steel pipe he was holding, inches from Frost's face. "We want your money and we want it now!"

Desperate situations often called for bizarre solutions, Frost concluded, and the bind they were in now was no exception. Wearing what he hoped was an expression of resigned defeat, the one-eyed man turned to his friend. "Did you ever see the old Hope and Crosby movies?"

The FBI agent wrinkled his forehead. "Wha . . . ?"

"You know—the 'Road' pictures—ever see any?"

"Yeah, yeah—I think so, but . . ."

"You remember how they used to get out of tough jams?"

11

"What all this talk?" the ringleader shouted, giving Frost a shove. "We want your money—now!"

"Do you remember, O'Hara—Hope and Crosby used the gag in every picture they made. Remember?"

A glimmer of recognition came to O'Hara's eyes. "Yeah, I remember. But jeez, Frost—you gotta be nuts to think . . ."

"Come on, O'Hara, be a sport. These guys want our money, so let's . . . Give Them the Money."

"You heard your friend," the ringleader was into shoving O'Hara now too. "Give us your money."

"Aww, nuts," O'Hara shook his head in despair as he shifted around to face Frost, leaning over into a crouch, bracing his hands on his knees as Frost began to chant the rhyme—both men clapping one another's hands at the appropriate time.

"Patty Cake, Patty Cake, Baker's Man," Frost chanted, "Give the Gang Our Money as Fast as We CAN!"

On the word "CAN" Frost and O'Hara snapped up from their crouched positions, Frost wheeling left, launching a double Tae Kwon Do kick with his right foot, the toe of his sixty-five dollar shoe impacting the Fat Cat leader's mouth. O'Hara's balled right fist slammed hard against a wiry, greasy-haired man holding a half-rusted chain.

"Damn!" the one-eyed man swore, his knuckles connecting painfully with the gang leader's bridgework, blood spouting from cracked and split lips as the stunned teddy boy swallowed broken pieces of his own blood-stained teeth and dropped, unconscious, to the ground.

Frost wrenched the steel pipe from the stricken gang leader's unfeeling grip, simultaneously shifting his body weight to the left. Catching a sudden movement from the corner of his right eye, Frost twisted, swinging the piece of steel pipe in his hands like a club, narrowly deflecting the downward rush of a similar piece of pipe aimed at his head. "Missed," he said, then stabbed out with a lightning fast jab, hammering into the unprotected groin of his foe—mashing both the man's testicles, crushing them against the apex of his thighs.

The injured man's screams were only starting to build as Frost whacked the man senseless up the side of the skull, then turned to confront a fresh wave of attackers. Close to a yard in length, the piece of pipe Frost held was weighted along its upper half with smaller pieces of pipe jammed inside. He put the top-heavy features of the pipe to good use, slashing out, its weighted end clipping the jaw—breaking it—of the knife-wielding gang member reaching him first.

Before Frost could pull back the pipe for another swing he heard himself cry out, a chain from one of the teddy boys slamming into his leg, coiling around the ankle of his right foot, threatening to jerk him off his feet, bring him down. He started falling, somehow catching his balance before that could happen, then struck out with the pipe at the forehead of the guy at the opposite end of the chain.

"Heads, you lose," Frost murmured, the weighted end of the deadly steel pipe caving in the front of his would-be killer's face with all the ease of a boot heel crushing a beer can, the man's ability to stand deflating like a punctured ballon.

Shaking free of the chain binding his ankle, Frost wheeled to the side, a short-bladed butterfly knife tearing at the fabric of his jacket, ripping away a section of the shirt Frost was wearing underneath, then continuing out again into open space. The one-eyed man frowned—the shirt and jacket both had been gifts to him from Bess.

Grabbing the wrist of the hand holding the butterfly

13

before it could get away, Frost twisted and pulled, yanking the arm back and straight, framing a perfect target for the piece of steel pipe which Frost sent, plowing into the arm with tremendous force, breaking the ulna.

Pushing the howling man between himself and the curved blade of another knife, Frost shot the sweat from his eye, hearing a whoosh of air to his right, turning in time to see a frenzied O'Hara—a four foot length of chain wrapped around his hand—whipping the chain across the faces and chests of a pair of teddy boys foolish enough to try rushing the lanky agent.

Frost saw one of the men drop his weapon, hands reaching for his head and the bloody stub of his missing left ear, while the second man made the mistake of remaining on his feet; O'Hara correcting that oversight with a vicious backswing of the chain that virtually lifted the man from his feet, sending him sailing through the fog-laden night air, to crash with a broken neck on the hard damp pavement.

"Not bad, Mike," Frost called.

"Beats the pants off feeling naked," came the terse reply.

In addition to the two men O'Hara had just taken down, plus two more bodies stretched out at the FBI agent's feet, Frost mentally calculated that, counting the teddy boys he had disposed of, the odds against them had considerably lessened—only about three-to-one now. Together, Frost realized, he and O'Hara had incapacitated better than half of the Fat Cat's original numbers—all in a brawl that, so far, had taken less than a minute!

Frost steadied himself, holding the piece of steel pipe in front of him in a double-handed grip, ready to confront his next obvious opponent—the same man whose knife Frost had blocked with the body of the

14

broken-armed loser using the butterfly. The man glared at Frost, the animal-hunger look in his eyes leaving little doubt in Frost's mind that he would like nothing more at that moment than the pleasure of carving a certain one-eyed mercenary to ribbons.

The man feinted with the blade to his left, telegraphed and deliberate, well out of range of Frost's steel pipe, testing the one-eyed man's reflexes. Frost remained where he was, rooted to the spot, turning slightly to the left to guard against an attack from another pair of teddy boys moving in for the kill. He tensed, the brick wall of the building behind him pressing at this shoulders, the yellowed glow from the street light above lending a ghostly hue to the surroundings. Another couple of seconds and they would be on him . . .

Whistles, Frost heard them and so did the others, cutting through the night, filtering along the dockside roadway, coming at them through the fog and darkness. Whistles—closer now—and then the sound of the running footsteps drawing near.

"*Jing-cha!*" the teddy boy squared off against Frost hissed from between clenched teeth. "*Jing-cha!*"

And as mysteriously as they had appeared, the gang of teddy boys vanished, taking the wounded, leaving the dead, slipping away to be lost in the fog.

"What do you make of that?" O'Hara asked, letting the chain slip from his fingers, crossing to where Frost stood. "Another gang, you think?" By now the shrieking whistles and advancing footsteps were less than fifty yards away.

"Another gang, yeah." Frost dropped the piece of steel pipe. "I think it's the police."

"Cripes! With half the Hong Kong teddy boy population sprawled at our feet, we'll be answering questions forever."

"Not if we make a break for it. Come on!"

15

Frost turned and ran, O'Hara right behind him—the pair of them running blindly—away from the direction of the approaching police.

"Ting-zhi!" came a shout of authority. "Stop!"

And then the shouts were lost as Frost and O'Hara, rounding a corner, found themselves running up a narrow street lined with closed-for-the-night warehouses, well in advance of their pursuers, reaching the end of the block just as a brightly lit car met them at the corner and stopped.

O'Hara grinned. "Well, I'll be a son-of-a..."

"A taxi!" Frost shouted. "Let's go!"

Running to the car as the back door of the cab popped open, Frost and O'Hara jumped inside, Frost slamming the door behind them.

"Great timing, mac," Frost told the driver. "Now, how's about stepping on the gas!"

The cab driver answered with a grunt, twisting on the front seat, turning so he faced the men in back—a Chinese Type 64 silenced pistol clamped in his fist, the business end of its barrel pointing at Frost's stomach.

"It is a pleasure and an honor to meet you, Captain Frost," the cabbie said, his English classroom perfect. "And you too, Agent O'Hara. I am the contact you were to meet tonight."

"Aw wow," Frost sighed, staring at the muzzle of the Type 64. "Wow."

"No, Captain. Ling Wao. Ah Wao is my nephew."

The one-eyed man glanced over to O'Hara and—quietly—said, "Wow, wow, wow..."

16

Chapter Two

The cobra did nothing as the expert snake-killer, a man roughly Frost's age—thirty-five or so—thrust his hands into the bamboo cage, skillfully snatching the cobra into the open air. Patting the poisonous snake's upper body to agitate it, the snake-killer watched respectfully as the cobra shot up its triangular neck, puffing up its hood, swollen and aggressive.

Smiling at Frost and the others, the snake-killer clutched the cobra by the neck then, stepping on its head and tail to prevent the reptile from wriggling free, took out a knife, quickly slitting the beast's belly, stopping at the incision to remove the delicacy of the bean-sized gall bladder. Then in one brilliant stroke with the tip of the knife, the snake was skinned from head to tail. Another flash of the blade and the cobra's head was removed, severed from its writhing body in a single cut from the knife—blood pouring from the wound in a crimson pool.

The blade chopped and chopped, slicing, dicing and shredding the snake meat, which was then taken from their table and carried to the restaurant's kitchen for preparation.

"The Cantonese have a saying, gentlemen: 'When the autumn winds blow, the three snakes are fat.' You are visiting Hong Kong during the best season for snake eating. You are, indeed, in for a treat."

"I'd rather be in for a quarter-pounder," O'Hara

17

admitted, Frost noting with amusement the blanched expression on his older friend's face.

"You must surrender to the moment," the man calling himself Ling Wao assured O'Hara. "You are certain to find the snake meat slices with chicken livers, which I have ordered for us, much to your liking."

Frost sipped at his drink—Seagrams Seven and ice with a splash of water—mentally trying to get a fix on their escort, the mysterious Mr. Ling. By his estimation Ling Wao was in his mid-forties, perhaps even fifty. He was a remarkably compact man, no more than five-feet six inches tall, with thin bony shoulders, and close-cropped jet black hair graying at the temples.

The clothes Ling wore—a dark brown tailored suit with matching shirt—while not as pedestrian as a government-issued uniform would have been, still shied enough on the lean side of extravagant to be labeled conservative.

But it was Ling's eyes, the traditional windows of the soul, which Frost found most interesting. They were the calculating eyes of a human machine, conditioned through the years, out of necessity, to record all and reveal nothing of the man's true emotions, serving always as a protective barrier between the man behind the mask of illusion and the world he lived in.

"Don't get us wrong, Mr. Ling," Frost said. "We appreciate your hospitality—the drinks are fine and I'm sure we're going to enjoy our dinner, but it's a little difficult for us to be over the moon about all of this when, less than fifteen minutes ago, you were pointing a gun at us."

"Ah," Ling Wao made a clicking noise at the back of his throat, "regrettably what you say is so, Captain Frost, and my only excuse, I am afraid, is that these are troubled times we live in, eh, and one does not bandy about taking chances when one does not need to. I

18

trained my weapon on you and Agent O'Hara only long enough to ascertain without a doubt that you were, indeed, the men I was supposed to meet.''

"And speaking of meeting us, sport," O'Hara complained, downing the last of the Myers's Rum from his glass. "Why the hell weren't you waiting for us down along the docks like you were supposed to?"

"The area of which you speak," Ling confided, "is notoriously known for its criminal element, especially after dark.''

O'Hara laughed, "No joke, pal. Me and Frost nearly got ourselves killed trying to track you down.''

"A mouse does not seek cheese in the lion's mouth."

"A wet bird never flies at night," Frost interjected.

"Which is why I let you find your way to me instead of the other way around,'' Ling continued, ignoring the interruption. "Were I to have followed such a foolish path and fallen into the hands of your teddy boy attackers and been robbed, possibly even slain, then, most regrettably, I would have been unavailable to relay the information I possess to you.''

"Meaning what?" Frost demanded. "We're sitting down in front of you here and now, and we expect some answers.''

"And you shall have them, Captain Frost. First, before we begin, I must know the extent of your knowledge regarding our conference this evening.''

"You could put it in a tea cup, Mr. Ling ...''

"Please." The Red Chinese agent of S.A.D.—Social Affairs Department, the Communist Chinese equivalent of the American C.I.A.—held up his hand. "If we are to work together as a team, then I believe it would be prudent to set formality aside. My first name is Wao. I would be honored if you would use that title when addressing me.''

"Sure, uh Wao," Frost returned, "anything you say.

19

You can call me Hank, and O'Hara sitting next to me, his first name is Mike. But back to what you just said, the part about us 'working as a team.' I don't know what black hat you're pulling all the facts from, friend, but believe me, you're getting them from a privileged source. O'Hara, that is, Mike and I were contacted by the American State Department yesterday morning. All we were told was that there was some hush-hush business brewing in your neighborhood that they wanted us to check out. That's it. The boys back home told us to pack our bags and fly to Hong Kong, check into a hotel, then scout around the area down by the docks at the time our meet with you was scheduled for tonight. Any further instructions we were to receive were to come directly from you."

"Correct," Ling nodded, "and I have been given the full assurance of your government representatives that, once my instructions have been made, you will follow them to the letter."

"Hey, wait a minute, Ling, Wing, or whatever your name really is." O'Hara slammed his empty glass down on the table. "I may have agreed to tag along with Frost on this scouting expedition we're on, but I'll be damned if I'm going to sit back fat and sassy while some lousy Commie S.O.B. calls the shots. You savvy that, mister?"

"I understand your attitude entirely, Mr. O'Hara. Your patriotic devotion to your nation is commendable. In all honesty I must confess that, if I were in your shoes, compelled to accepting orders from a ranking member of the opposition party, then I, too, would voice my protests."

"I ain't just talking, sport. No Commie's telling me what to do. Period."

Instead of taking what O'Hara had said personally, apparently, Ling calmly sipped at his drink of hot ginseng laced with honey. "I accept your words at their face value, Mr. O'Hara. And no offense is taken. That we are cast as players on opposing sides is but a whim of fate, an accident of birth. You and Captain Frost could have been born Chinese, while, had the fates so willed, my birthplace might have been in your American city of Chicago. But discussions of what could have been are not for men as us. Like it or not, we are all realists bound by immutable rules and regulations."

"And at this point in time," Frost interjected, "the rules call for the three of us to meet on equal ground?"

"Precisely, Captain. And the reason the rules have been changed are directly linked to my nation's deteriorating relationship with the Soviet Union."

"I know exactly what you mean, Wao." Frost pulled a fresh Camel from the pack in his pocket, lighting the cigarette in the blue-yellow flame of the battered Zippo. "If you want to know the truth, my ties with the Russians haven't been too hot lately, either."*

"Then you may appreciate more fully what the faltering Sino-Soviet attitudes portend should they continue as they have on their present course."

The one-eyed man regarded Ling intently. "I'm sure there are those who insist that the bad vibes between China and Russia could eventually serve as the catalyst to trigger World War III."

"Exactly," Ling agreed. "And it is this likelihood of eventual war between China and Russia that has brought about an interesting consideration—the probable alliance between the United States and China in the form of a mutual defense pact."

"Now I've heard everything," O'Hara groaned, ordering a refill on his drink from a passing waiter. "The next thing you'll be telling me is that all of us

*See, THEY CALL ME THE MERCENARY #14, The Siberian Alternative

21

back in the States will have to take compulsory Chinese lessons."

"Nothing so radical, I assure you, Agent O'Hara. But as a choice—that of siding with the lesser of two evils, China versus the Soviet Union—the attraction of such a proposal has met with the favor of your government."

"So, how does that tie in with our being here?" Frost asked.

Ling waited for the waiter bringing O'Hara his drink to depart then continued. "Earlier this week a special American emissary, a man named Bruce Thoresen, was in Peking, on behalf of the United States, negotiating just such a proposal."

"And there was trouble," Frost guessed.

"An unqualified disaster," Ling responded. "Given the sensitive nature of the negotiations, stringent security precautions were put into effect. Unfortunately, they were not sufficient to deter the pro-Soviet reactionary terrorist elements within my country. Somehow the terrorists learned of the negotiations and where they were taking place. The conference was attacked and, in the ensuing battle which followed, the men bodyguarding the emissary were all murdered, the American, Bruce Thoresen, kidnapped.

"We can only surmise the true reason for Thoresen's kidnapping, but both my government and yours have reached the conclusion that Thoresen will most likely be starved, beaten, drugged—whatever it takes to force him to write a detailed description of the negotiations—and that the induced statement will then be released to the world press."

"At which point the crap hits the fan," Frost said.

"Such a disclosure," Ling confided, "could only serve to damage U.S. relations with Russia, could even bring the world to the brink of the global nuclear war some seem so determined to have. At any rate, such a

22

disclosure would doubtless precipitate border warfare on the Sino-Soviet boundary."

Frost considered the importance of what Ling was saying. International tensions being what they were, he knew it could easily take far less than the disclosure of the Sino-American defense pact negotiations for hostilities to reach a boil. "Tell me what happened when the United States was informed of the kidnapping."

"Understandably, your government insisted on being personally involved in the case. My government agreed to the demand, limiting, however, American involvement to that of a member of your Justice Department, plus one counter-terrorist specialist. That's where you and Agent O'Hara entered the picture, and now that you have joined me here in Hong Kong, we shall soon embark upon the mission at hand—finding and rescuing Mr. Thoresen."

O'Hara swallowed a gulp of his Myers's Rum, then leaned across the table. "And how soon is it before this little jaunt of ours is due to get underway?"

"Plans," Ling told them, "call for a departure to mainland China in twelve hours time. Your weapons and gear will be waiting for you once we arrive, as will any and all assistance you may require. Once we have assembled on the mainland our search for Thoresen will begin."

Frost took a final puff on his cigarette, inhaling the smoke slowly and letting it out, then snuffed the rest of the Camel in a nearby ashtray. "You say that 'our' search for Thoresen will begin—does that mean you are to accompany us to China?"

Ling Wao's only reply was a curt nod.

"Yeah, well I don't care whether you like it one way or the other," O'Hara informed the Chinese agent, "but it's going to take more meat on my plate than you've dished up to convince me that everything you've

23

told us is the truth. After all, face it, you're a, ah..."

"Communist," Ling said the word.

"Yeah," O'Hara went on, "a Communist. Now, if Thoresen really was kidnapped like you say, despite all your so-called stringent security precautions, then somebody on your end of the rope obviously slipped up. That equates to a leak in the dike—somebody with a big mouth or else a compromised position. In short, one of the pro-Soviet fanatics you claim are responsible for the kidnapping has infiltrated your Social Affairs Department. Cripes, the spy could even be you. Uh uh, I can't speak for Frost, here, but unless you can come up with something more substantial than a simple sayso from you, then you ain't getting my cooperation for anything—not even the time of day."

Ling finished drinking his tea, speaking as he set the empty cup down. "I anticipated your desire for additional verification, Agent O'Hara. Presented with the same set of circumstances now placed before you, I would also want further proof. To that end, after we have dined I shall be happy to transport you and Captain Frost to the American Embassy. There you will have all the proof you need."

"Don't bet on it," O'Hara wasn't convinced. "Right, Hank?"

The one-eyed man said to his friend, after spotting a pair of tray-bearing waiters heading their way, "We'll know after dinner, Mike. And speaking of chow, here comes the old snake in the grass right now..."

Chapter Three

"I think I need a seltzer," O'Hara told Frost as they watched Ling Wao and his "taxi" disappear around a corner. The Communist Chinese agent had wished them well, apologized for not going in with them, then left the pair standing in front of the U.S. Embassy.

"I trust that by visiting the American Embassy your curiosity will be satisfied and that we will be working together," the slightly built Ling had said as they stepped from the cab. "However, if the fates have deemed otherwise, please accept my gratitude for an evening well spent. Farewell." Then he had waved good-bye, put the car into gear, and was gone.

"You don't need a seltzer," the one-eyed man grinned as they turned on their heels and made their way to the front gates leading to the entrance of the Embassy. "You only think you do."

"My ass! Cobra and chicken livers—my stomach's killing me."

"Forget it, Mike. If your stomach made it through that mess in Canada okay, there's no reason why it can't handle a little exotic food."*

"The way my gut feels right now makes that stint in Canada seem like a piece of cake. It was all I could do to look at the slop without dropping the whole nine yards right there in the restaurant. And you had two helpings

*See, THEY CALL ME THE MERCENARY #5, Canadian Killing Ground

25

of the stuff."

"I thought it was pretty tasty."

"You ain't human, Frost."

They were challenged at the gates by a young Marine guard requesting the nature of their business at the Embassy.

"Are you aware of the late hour, gentlemen?" The guard stood before them, M-16 held ready, blocking the entrance through the gates. "It's nearly Oh-One-Hundred—hardly a proper time for conducting business. I'm afraid you will have to wait until the ..."

"Listen, sonny," O'Hara growled, Frost guessing the miserable condition of his upset stomach adding anger to his already sour attitude. "I'm Special Agent Mike O'Hara with the FBI. The guy next to me is Captain Hank Frost." O'Hara produced his identification for the guard to see. "We've come a long way to have a confab with the Ambassador and there's no way we're going to wait until the sun's up to have it. You got that? I'm giving ya sixty seconds to clear us with a senior officer, then we're coming through—with or without your approval."

Their clearance arrived with seconds to spare and five minutes later they were sitting across from a visibly agitated—and sleepy—Charge-de-Affaires.

"I hope you have a good explanation for disturbing my night's sleep, O'Hara," the Ambassador said. His full name was Winston Ward III, he was middle-aged and slightly paunchy, and—Frost noted—was wearing a silk dressing gown nicer than anything Bess had back home in Atlanta. "You men are hardly following the channels of protocol by barging in on me like this."

"Stuff protocol," O'Hara snapped back, then thought better of it and added a half-hearted, "Sir. But we have questions of international importance, and the answers couldn't wait till morning."

26

"Oh, all right." Ambassador Ward settled down into a plush cushioned easy chair, folded his arms in his lap, and crossed his legs. "What are these questions that couldn't wait until morning?"

And O'Hara explained to him—telling the Ambassador everything—from the State Department request that they come to Hong Kong, about their confrontation earlier that evening with the Fat Cats, and of their meeting and conversation with Ling Wao. O'Hara ended by telling the Ambassador that the only reason he and Frost had come to the Embassy was to determine, somehow, the legitimacy of Ling Wao's fantastic story.

Having listened to O'Hara without interruption, Ambassador Ward politely excused himself and left the room—ostensibly to make what he categorized as "several phone calls to the powers that be." He returned seven-and-a-half minutes later, his previous expression of sleepy resentment replaced with one of total concern.

"Well?" O'Hara said, he and Frost standing when the Ambassador re-entered the room. "What's the good word?"

"Not to your liking, I'm afraid. I have just verified that everything your Mr. Ling Wao told you is true. Apparently, you and Captain Frost will be leaving for mainland China in the morning."

Thunder rumbled—audibly—across O'Hara's belly and he muttered, "Cobras and chicken livers ..."

"What?" the Ambassador asked.

"Nothing," Frost supplied. "By the way—you wouldn't happen to have any seltzer handy?"

Chapter Four

It was named the *Kuai-yu*, the *Fast Fish*, and as the motorized junk began its journey—threading through the congested traffic of sampans by the hundreds, traditional Chinese junks with their torn and colorful bat-wing sails, modern naval vessels, cargo-weighted freighters, as well as ocean liners and ferryboats—Hank Frost stood on the upper deck of the *Fast Fish*, viewing the motorized junk's progress with a small sense of awe.

"Amazing," the one-eyed man concluded. "Amazing."

Long considered one of the three finest and most beautiful harbors of the world, its seventeen square miles of natural anchorage provided the ideal setting for exporting better than two and one-half million dollars worth of goods per day. Coupling that statistic with the knowledge that Hong Kong residents consumed more than 6,000 pigs, 100,000 chickens, 1,000 metric tons of rice, 1,200 metric tons of vegetables, and 300 metric tons of fish each and every day of the year—most of which entered Hong Kong via the harbor—and you had the makings of a logistical nightmare. Even after Ling Wao, now serving as First Officer on the *Fast Fish*, had relayed that information to him, Frost had found the staggering figures difficult to believe.

What he could relate to, though, was the fact that he and O'Hara were leaving Hong Kong behind them now and embarking upon a search whose outcome was completely unknown. Following their meeting with

Ambassador Ward at the American Embassy, Frost and O'Hara had returned to their hotel, courtesy of a ride provided by Uncle Sam, there to make the most of what remained of the night and try to get some sleep.

O'Hara had nodded off at once, slept like a log, upset stomach and all, snoring like a buzz saw most of the night. Frost's fortune with the down time was another story altogether; the total amount of sleep he'd managed to get measuring minutes, rather than hours. And not because of O'Hara's raucous snoring either. If he had chosen to, Frost could have taken a nap in the middle of the Super Bowl.

No, the reason for Frost's disquiet ran deeper than that, he realized. As a man long used to the rigors and stress of extended combat campaigns, the one-eyed mercenary had acquired years ago the enviable skill of being able to sleep at will. "Sleep when you can, where you can," had been his credo for longer than he cared to think about. "You never know when you'll have another chance."

So why, he wondered, had sleep eluded him? Bess perhaps? Frost wasn't sure. Beginning with the first day they had met, he and Bess had shared so much.* Danger, death, sorrow and love—most of all love. Bess Stallman was the most incredible woman he had ever known. Where was the problem, then? Marriage? They had discussed it often enough, had even gone so far as to get an apartment together in Atlanta. But as much as he loved her, Frost wasn't ready yet to take the next big plunge, the one leading to the altar.

Was it fear holding him back? A private fear that if he did marry Bess, then his life as he was conditioned to living it would cease to exist? And if he did call it quits, putting away his guns and knives and globehopping escapades forever, would that be so terrible?

*See, THEY CALL ME MERCENARY #1, The Killer Genesis

Maybe so. Like anyone foolish enough to take up his profession and stick with it, the one-eyed merc had made his fair share of enemies over the years. Most of them were dead, some were not, and Frost had nearly discovered the hard way that if his enemies couldn't get to him one way or another, they'd be more than happy to accept Bess as a convenient substitute.* ** It was an easy way of killing the man by damning his spirit—living with the hell of knowing someone close to him had died in his place.

Frost didn't have the right to ask Bess to share that kind of existence—a life where an act as simple as a knock at the front door could be the paperboy coming to collect, or else some crackpot from Frost's past with an ax to grind. There was too much violent uncertainty in his life for a marriage to work. Yet, knowing all that, Bess still wanted him, to unite and build a life together, and to hell with the dangers. Maybe she was crazy. Maybe they both were, Frost didn't know. The endless possibilities played over and over in his mind, again and again. Until finally he had slept. And dreamed. But not for long . . .

"It doesn't surprise me, Frost."

"What's that?"

"About Hong Kong."

"Hong Kong."

"That's right. Internationally, it's rated as the Number One spy center. Some honor, huh? And all because that hunk of rock and humanity is sittin' on China's doorstep. Holy . . ."

"So, what is it about Hong Kong that doesn't surprise you?"

"What? Oh, yeah—well, seeing as how we are in the

---

*See, THEY CALL ME THE MERCENARY #9, The Terror Contract
**See, THEY CALL ME THE MERCENARY #10, Bush Warfare

Number One spy capital of the world, it's no small wonder to me how we've been suckered into working with the Reds. You dance in crap, some of it's bound to stick to your shoes."

"Somebody on our side must have liked the idea, Mike, otherwise you and I would still be back in the States. I could be out taking in a movie with Bess. You could be at home polishing your badge."

"Aww, gimme a break. A little gung ho fever now and then is good for the soul."

"Forget it, O'Hara. I'm not razzing ya. I'm just as jazzed about working with Ling Wao and his band of Red rice eaters as I would be hearing that Papa Yuri is my long lost uncle. You and I both hate it, but that doesn't change a thing: There's an American somewhere in China in deep-shit trouble, and it's fallen into our laps to see about bailing him out."

They watched in silence then as prominent landmarks were met, observed, and left behind in the slow spreading wake of the *Fast Fish*. Kawloon Peninsula, seen across the harbor at the onset of their journey, surrounded by an impressive range of hills resembling a series of dragons, Stonecutter's Island, Tsing Yi Island, around Lantau Island, then on to where Castle Peak overlooked their progress from a height of 1,913 feet—all the while their motorized junk plowing lazily through the water, making for a place called Deep Bay and the mouth of the Sham Chun River nearby. Once there they would weigh anchor, ride a sampan ashore, and be met on the beach by a helicopter from the Communist Chinese Air Force. Neither Frost nor O'Hara had been told where the chopper would take them . . .

They were rounding the end of Castle Peak Bay, turning into the curve that would put them in line with the mainland, when the *Fast Fish* was attacked. Frost, standing alone at the junk's starboard quarter, his eye

31

squinting against the reflected glare of the water, saw it first—beginning as a faraway speck on South China Sea, gradually expanding in size until there was no mistaking his sighting. It was a gasoline powered launch, approaching full speed from the rear, threatening to overtake the *Fast Fish* in a matter of minutes. Not only that, the one-eyed man observed, but even over the rapidly dwindling distance separating the two vessels, he could make out a twin battery of heavy caliber machine guns, mounted turret-style, aboard the launch—one on the bridge deck, the second placed on the foredeck or whatever you called it.

"Ling!" Frost screamed at the top of his voice, running across the side deck to alert Wao and everyone else. "We got trouble ..."

"Right here in River City," O'Hara chimed in, hurrying over to where Frost and Ling were already engaged in excited conversation.

"We're gonna to have company." Frost pointed in the direction of the swiftly gaining launch, now less than twenty-five hundred yards away and closing.

"Sheesh," O'Hara said, shielding his eyes against the glare for a look. "And they seem to be packin' some muscle."

"My guess is Browning 50s, and they've got at least two of 'em." Frost turned to Ling. "Any chance of out-running her, maybe making it to shore?"

Ling grimly shook his head. "Our transport, unfortunately, is fast in name only. The speeding launch will easily overtake us. We have no choice but to fight."

"With what?" Frost scanned the principally bare deck of the junk. "Shouts and insults? They'll rip us to ribbons."

Ling shouted something in Chinese to one of the six crewmen manning the *Fast Fish*—the sailor nodding once, then vanishing through the companionway hatch to the cargo hold below. "I concede that our enemy has the power to destroy us, Captain Frost, but our foes may discover that wishing for something is not always the same as having that wish fulfilled."

O'Hara shot Frost a pained look. "All of a sudden I feel naked again."

Frost grabbed a pair of binoculars from the seaman standing nearest him and watched the launch bearing down on them, less than a mile away, cutting smoothly through the water, chasing them down. His palms felt itchy and damp and his mouth tasted dry. Even if they jumped into the water to avoid taking a direct hit with the 50s—they were Brownings, he was sure of that now—all the launch had to do was criss-cross the area a few times to catch them in her engines, and just like magic, they'd all become fish food.

"Listen, Ling!" Frost exclaimed. "If you've got anything up your sleeves besides elbows, now would be a good time to tell us. A few more seconds we'll be within range and then we'll be gone like there's no to-Mao . . ."

Ling ignored the ill-timed bid for humor. "While it is true that the brunt of my duties with S.A.D. have kept me immune from such confrontations as we seemed destined to participate in, it is also true that I have long been a practitioner of your American Boy Scout motto: Be Prepared."

An exasperated O'Hara shouted, throwing his arms out wide. "You call this being prepared? You're outta your friggin' . . ."

"Gentlemen, please!" Ling held out his hand as the sailor who had gone below returned; and not, Frost noted with more than a mild sense of relief, empty-handed. "Your weapons. Take all you want, but use all you take. Good luck."

Frost didn't need a second invitation, rushing to the sailor's side, coming away with a Chinese Type 56 version of the popular-with-terrorists assault rifle, the Soviet AKM. Frost hefted the mid-weight nine pound rifle into his hands, checking to make sure its 30-round magazine was fully seated, then used his right thumb to depress the safety all the way down—fully automatic.

All about him, with the exception of the junk's pilot, who was doing his best to make the *Fast Fish* fly, the rest of the crew, including O'Hara and Ling, were going through the same motions with their weapons. Frost reached into a burlap sack which suddenly appeared at his feet, whipping out three spare magazines for himself, plus two extra which he tossed to O'Hara. The launch was under a half-mile from them now, well within range, but obviously intending to move in closer and make their 'easy-kill' with the Brownings all that more spectacular.

"We have to hit the gunners on the first couple of sweeps." Frost hollered across the deck to Ling, "or the 50s they're using will make chopsticks outta the *Fast Fish* and us too! It's gonna be tough. The gunners are both armor-protected up to their shoulders, and they can rotate their Brownings a full 180 degrees as they pass, coming up beside us. It looks like they're moving in closer than they have to, which is good for us. That lets us keep our shots in tighter groupings. If they wise up and opt for maintaining a safer distance, though, it's our ass. They'll be able to hit us without worrying about us hitting back."

Ling replied with something sounding to Frost like, "We shall see," then turned to a pair of his sailors, ordering them in Chinese to fetch something else from the cargo hold.

Frost, seeing the sailors disappear below, shouted to Ling. "Another surprise?"

But he only smiled, fixing his eyes on a position beyond Frost's shoulder, out over the water. Frost

34

turned, his one eye following the path of Ling's gaze, the cotton-dryness in his mouth an intolerable nuisance. The enemy launch was running parallel with them now, her twin mounted Brownings swinging hard to port, ready to gun them down. Frost tried to swallow and couldn't, then stole a glance to his left where O'Hara, fifteen feet further down the deck, was engaged in lining up the sights of his rifle with the gunner's positions on the launch. Frost whistled to get Mike's attention, got it, then gave his friend a 'thumbs-up' sign with his left hand. The older O'Hara returned the gesture, sinking below the barrier of the junk's wooden sides as the enemy opened fire, both powerful Brownings cutting a dangerous trail across the *Fast Fish*, from bow to stern.

Frost barely had the time to plaster himself to the deck as bullets from the booming Browning machineguns blew softball-sized chunks out of the junk, mere inches above his head. He waited for the raking gunfire to cease, splinters of wood pelting the back of his neck and head, covering his face—he shielded his eye. The bullets passed, moving on, the one-eyed man climbing to one knee, aiming over the rail, finger twitching on the Type 56's two-stage trigger, sending ten three-round bursts of the 7.62 x 39mm 123-grain bullets targeting in on the enemy launch's gunsites. Then he was down, falling back to the deck, dumping out the spent magazine, inserting a fresh stick when the Browning opened up again, slugs starting at opposing ends of the junk, chewing their way along the deck, converging in the middle.

Screams then, horrible sounding. Frost spinning, seeing it all: blood spurting from a splinter wound, throat wound, one of the crewmen—a boy, perhaps nineteen—the kid losing control, screaming again, jumping to his feet, clawing for the wooden dagger piercing his neck, hands flopping uselessly in the air, dropping to his sides, the Brownings seeking him out, both 50s stitching him open in a splattering explosion, flopping the body across the deck and into the sea, both Brownings suddenly silent.

The side of the junk facing the attack—as much as three feet above the deck in some places—resembled an oak-colored slice of Swiss cheese to Frost as he and everyone else answered the Browning's onslaught with fire-power of their own. Sweat stinging his right eye, Frost took position, aimed and fired, squeezing the trigger with its smooth seven pound pull, again and again, shooting between the junk and the launch, emptying the magazine, going for broke, one of his .30 caliber slugs finding its mark, scoring with a paydirt hit to the exposed head of the gunner manning the bridge deck gun.

"Ha!" Frost grinned, the body of the dead gunner slipping from sight, a second terrorist appearing through the sliding door onto the cockpit, crawling on all fours, making for the ladder leading to the bridge, hands gripping the ladder, feet flying, climbing it, racing for the unmanned Browning, then one shot, two shots, three shots more, O'Hara's rifle barking in his hands, striking the terrorist, killing him, hanging him from the ladder like a side of butchered beef.

"Hey, whatta ya think of that, Frost?" O'Hara smile was ear to ear. "Not bad shootin' for a ten pound popgun."

"I've seen better," Frost joked, then frowned—the launch was revving her engines, beginning to pull away to starboard, to the right. "That's what I was afraid of," he said to Ling. "They're gonna move out far enough so we can't hit 'em, then cut back in with the Brownings again. The greater range'll work to their advantage. They'll be able to mow us down without a scratch. Damn! If I thought we could get away with it I'd say

36

chase 'em, herd 'em in to shore. But that's impossible. We're not built for speed and those 50s of theirs would chop us to bits."

The two sailors Ling had ordered to the cargo hold before the shooting had started suddenly reappeared, carrying between them the pieces to a weapon.

"Holy shit!" the one-eyed man whispered.

"You like it?" Ling asked.

Frost laughed. "Does a chicken have . . . ?"

Before Frost could finish his question the Browning mounted on the launch's foredeck came to life, its 50s guided home by each fifty-round tracer from the gun in a direct line leading to the sailors emerging from the hold. Ling frantically signaled for the men to take cover, but his warning came too late. The first man perished in a hailstorm of bullets, working his body apart in a half-inch meat grinder of pure destruction, while the second doomed sailor was diving to the deck when a single tracer round struck him in the face.

The Browning was lacing a confident pattern of death all about him as Frost began inching, crawling across the deck on his stomach, arms outstretched, his hands reaching for the pieces to the weapon the sailors had dropped. Then more bad news. He had his fingers on the weapon's tripod when the rate of Browning 50s striking the *Fast Fish*, threatening to turn the junk into scrap, suddenly doubled—telling Frost that the Browning atop the bridge deck had been remanned and had joined the fight again. It was now or never. If he didn't get the weapon together somehow and use it, they would all be dead thanks to the Brownings.

As O'Hara, Ling, and the remaining sailors gave him all the cover fire they could manage, without making themselves open targets, the one-eyed man rolled the tripod onto its legs, then reached out for the weapon that went with it, fingers grasping it, pulling it near, then grabbing, hefting its thirty-pound weight onto the tripod, locking it into place.

The weapon was a Soviet AGS-17 30mm grenade launcher with a full thirty-round magazine, each high-explosive fragmentation round, weighing 300 to 400 grams, and incorporating the A-1X-1 standard compound of 94 percent RDG and six percent wax. For Frost, fed up by now with the results of the Chi-com issued assault rifles against the superior firepower of the launch, the Soviet AGS-17 was just what the doctor ordered.

Scooting the grenade launcher across the deck, stopping at an open space on the side of the junk where the 50s had had a field day, Frost moved into position behind the AGS-17, released its safety, eased his hands over its black t-shaped grips, lined up on the launch and opened fire. With an estimated range of anywhere from 600 to 1,200 meters, and a cyclic rate of 300 rounds per minute, the one-eyed man directed his line of attack at the port side of the enemy launch, his first shots going high, correcting his aim, the Brownings on the launch locking onto his position, homing in on him, moving in for the kill, fighting to silence him and the AGS-17. Frost's ears, stinging from the constant barrage of gunfire, shaking his head, clearing his thoughts, correcting his aim again, still firing, better now—one, two, three, then another pair of the AGS-17's HEAT grenades hitting, detonating, bisecting the launch from bow to stern, the magazine in the grenade launcher running dry.

Frost squinted, wiping a bead of sweat from his eye, smoke and flame visible on the launch now, men screaming, clothes aflame, leaping into the water, the sides of the launch rupturing, exploding, a monstrous ball of orange and red fire rising into the air as the launch disintegrated, spewing rubble and death over the sea.

Realizing that he had been holding his breath, the one-eyed man stood, taking great gulps of air into his lungs. Alive—they had met the attack and survived. And didn't that feel good?

"Nice shootin', Frost." O'Hara came over to congratulate him with a friendly slap on the back.

"Thanks," Frost said, then turned to Ling, pointing down to the AGS-17 on the deck at their feet. "Nice rig, Ling. A rare one. It's probably one of the few pieces of gear the Soviets haven't gotten around to exporting yet. I don't suppose you'd like to tell me how you came to have it?"

"A friend of a friend of a friend," Ling answered, then excused himself to go and assess the damages incurred during the attack.

"So much for the *Fast Fish*," O'Hara said after Ling had left. "The junk's been junked. Ha!"

"Very funny. All this excitement's worked up my appetite. I'm hungry."

"Hey, good idea, Frost. Me, too. What do you have in mind?"

The one-eyed man grinned. "Anything but junk food . . ."

Chapter Five

Their wait on the beach near the mouth of the Sham Chun River was short and sweet, Frost able to shake the sand out of his sixty-five dollar shoes and put them back on just as the Bell Model 222 Executive helicopter arrived for the first leg of their journey inland. The chopper stayed on the ground long enough for Frost, O'Hara and Ling, running and ducking low beneath the still-beating rotor blades, to climb aboard and hurriedly find seats. Seconds later the side door to the Bell, with the words Happy Time Air stenciled on it, was closed and latched shut, the pilot shouted something to Ling which sounded suspiciously like "Okey-Dokey," and then they were airborne—pulling swiftly into the clear blue of the morning sky, climbing to an announced cruising altitude of 8000 feet before leveling off on a north by northwest heading as best Frost could determine.

Frost, his stomach held in limbo somewhere between the inside of the chopper and the ground far below, was having trouble coming up with a single good reason why anyone in their right mind would like flying, when O'Hara leaned over to speak.

"They may be Reds and Commies, Frost, but they damn well sure know how to treat special people like us." He eyeballed the Bell Executive's plush interior. "Yes, sir, first class service for first class help. I'm not ashamed to admit we deserve it. Couldn't happen to a nicer bunch of guys."

Frost didn't get a chance to reply as Ling, excusing himself for the interruption, informed them of their initial destination—a little-used airfield in the Guangdong region, several miles out of Canton.

"There we will land and transfer to the plane which will fly us to Beijing."

O'Hara repeated, "Bay-Jing?"

"It's what we call Peking," Frost answered.

"Excellent guess, Captain Frost."

"Not a guess, Ling. I remember that tidbit of information from an old American television program."

"Ah," Ling smiled, lowering his chin to his chest, hunching up the shoulders of his slight frame, and announcing in a voice much deeper than his own, "Book him!" After which he regained his composure and confessed. "I am not totally unfamiliar with the comings and goings of your pastimes in the United States, Captain Frost—especially your American TV. Ben, Adam, and Horse . . ."

"The name is Hoss," O'Hara corrected.

"And Hoss, thank you. These names, as you can see, are quite well known to me."

"Okay if I smoke?" Frost asked, reaching for the crumpled pack of Camels in his pocket, waiting for Ling's assurance that it was safe to do so, then lighting one of the cigarettes with the blue-yellow flame of his Zippo. He inhaled the smoke deep into his lungs, holding it there before slowly exhaling. "That's better."

"I am curious, Captain Frost."

"What's that, Ling?"

"Your package of cigarettes with the desert animal on the front—may I examine it?"

"Sure." Frost fished the pack from his pocket and passed it over.

"Thank you." Ling Wao uncrumpled the pack and

41

read from the warning printed on its side. "Your American Surgeon General has determined that smoking cigarettes is hazardous to one's health."

"And he probably spent millions of taxpayer's money to make that conclusion, too. Go on."

"What I am curious about, Captain, is this: If the Surgeon General of the United States—a bonafide representative of your government—thinks sufficiently of the hazards of smoking tobacco to print his personal message to you on every pack, then how can you, in clear conscience as a loyal American, continue to smoke and pollute your body? Aren't you bound to follow your leaders?"

"Not when it comes to a personal vice like smoking cigarettes. I can smoke them if I want. It's my decision, one I make of my own free will. In America that's part of what's called 'Freedom of Choice.' "

"But that is not so different than in China. We too have the 'Freedom of Choice' to accept the dictates of our leaders."

"Um hmm," Frost said, "And what happens in China when you elect to exercise that 'Freedom of Choice' option and refuse to accept your leader's dictates?"

Ling Wao blinked, surprised at such a silly question. "The answer is simple, of course, Captain Frost. You lose your 'Choice of Freedom' . . ."

Twenty minutes later the Bell 222 Executive seemed to drop from the sky, plummeting like a rock to the ground—leaving Frost's stomach lost in the clouds—then making a cushion-soft landing on the airfield outside of Canton, touching down next to the plane that would fly them to Peking.

They disembarked, moving well away from the Bell's spinning rotor blades, then watched as the 222 Executive lifted off again and was gone. Communist Chinese soldiers—all wearing their ubiquitous dark green uniforms with red-barred collars, and matching hats with red stars in the center, all carrying the same Type 56 assault rifle which had been used in the battle aboard the *Fast Fish*—were lined up along the perimeter of the airstrip, facing out, weapons ready, in anticipation of a possible attack. Seeing so many of the Red Chinese soldiers at once made Frost's toes involuntarily curl up in his sixty-five dollar shoes. If anyone had told him a week ago that he would be working hand-in-hand with the Communist Chinese on a mission, he would have told them flat out that they were nuts. The funny part of it was, though, he would have been wrong.

"Come, gentlemen," Ling said once the chopper had lifted off. "Our flight awaits."

"Oh, no." O'Hara had taken two steps and stopped dead on his feet, his eyes staring in dismay at the aircraft Ling was leading them to. "It'll never get off the ground."

"What?" Hating flying as much as he did, Frost was anxious to hear more.

"I know that plane, Hank. It's a Martin 4-0-4, made sometime back around 1951-52. I thought there was only about a dozen of them left in service, but it looks like this here is number thirteen."

"Knock it off, O'Hara. You're just being superstitious."

"The hell I am. A prototype of the 4-0-4 was tested in '47. A year later one of 'em went down; 'a weakness in the wing structure' was what the investigators found. And here we are about to go up in one. Wilbur and Orville never had it so bad."

"That problem with the wing structure has to have been corrected," Frost told his friend, then turned to Ling. "Right, Wao?"

"Of course. The People's Republic of China has the third largest Air Force in the world. Having us transported to Beijing in an unsafe aircraft is unthinkable. Besides, I know this plane. I have flown in it on more than one occasion. The Mayo-Gwantsi is a plane you can trust."

"May-Oh-Gwan-See?" Frost repeated the name. "What's it mean?"

Ling searched for the phrase. "In English you would say, 'No Sweat.'"

"No Sweat," Frost rolled the name around on his tongue. "See, O'Hara? All that worrying over nothing. If we make it we'll be okay. If we don't, it won't matter. Right?"

"Yeah, okay." O'Hara reluctantly shuffled forward. "But only if I get a window seat..."

Miraculously, according to a sweating O'Hara at the time, the Mayo-Gwantsi didn't crash during take off, but instead managed to climb with apparent ease to 14,500 feet—the optimum altitude for maximum speed. Even with the Pratt and Whitney R-2800-CB16 Double Wasp radial piston engines pulling them through the air at 312 miles per hour, the flight to Peking would take the better part of four-and-one-half hours to complete.

Once they had settled into level flight, Ling led Frost and O'Hara to a cargo area at the back of the plane. "So you wouldn't feel entirely homesick, your government arranged for the delivery of this CARE package." Then he drew back a canvas tarp from over a large wooden crate and stepped aside, allowing Frost and O'Hara to pore over the crate's contents.

The crate contained their weapons. Not simply duplicates, but all of the originals they had left in the U.S. before flying to Hong Kong.

"Oh, baby, come to Daddy." O'Hara scooped his Smith & Wesson Metalifed and Mag-Na-Ported Model-29 .44 Magnum with its Cattle Baron leather shoulder holster out of the crate, then dug around until he could find its companion piece—a S&W Model 60 .38 Chief's Special stainless revolver, and the Cobra ankle holster that went with it. He stepped away from the crate to inspect the two guns and put them on.

First Frost removed the Interdynamics KG-99 9mm assault pistol, with sling and flash suppressor in place, along with three thirty-six round magazines. Next came the Gerber MkI boot knife, which he usually wore concealed in a sheath at the small of his back, then finally his pride and joy—the Browning 9mm High Power.

Frost hefted the weight of the gun in his hand, for the umpteenth time admiring its superb craftsmanship. Originally, he had used what was basically a stock version of the High Power, but when that one disappeared after his kidnapping by the KGB, it was time for him to go shopping.* And for Frost—depending so often on the versatility of the High Power to save his skin—there was only one place to go.

Contacting his pal Ron Mahovsky, head-honcho of Metalife Industries in Reno, Pennsylvania, Frost had been persuaded to forego getting another of the stock High Powers in favor of a customized version which Mahovsky agreed to fabricate for him. Frost didn't balk at the offer. Ron was an expert's expert when it came to firearms, and if he was willing to put together something special, then Frost was more than willing to give Ron the green light.

That "something special" was the High Power Frost now held. For openers Mahovsky had given the pistol the brushed stainless steel look of the Metalife SS Chromium M process. There was a custom, ambidextrous, slightly built up thumb safety, then a slide stop—larger than on the standard model, but not overly so,

*See, THEY CALL ME THE MERCENARY #14, The Siberian Alternative

45

designed for a firm feel when it was worked.

Sporting the Browning adjustable rear sight and higher profile front sight, Mahovsky had white outlined the rear sight blade notch and placed what Frost suspected as being a Smith & Wesson red ramp insert into the front sight. Aside from three new thirteen round magazines to go with the gun, there were two twenty-round extension magazines as well—these Metalifed, too.

Frost removed his jacket then reached into the wooden crate for his Cobra Comvest, which he slipped on into place. He took one of the thirteen round magazines, loaded as always with 115-grain hollow points, rammed the magazine up the High Power's well, his fist wrapped around the black checkered rubber Pachmayr grips. With the hammer down over the just chambered round, he eased the Browning into the Comvest shoulder holster, then slipped back into his jacket.

"Not feeling naked now are you, Mike?" Frost asked as O'Hara returned, the smile on his face worse than that of the proverbial kid in a candy store.

O'Hara rolled his shoulders and tugged at the lapels of his coat. "I tell ya, Frost, I feel great. Somebody tries any bullshit with us now, and I'll be ready for 'em!"

Which was when Ling signaled to them both that he would like a word with them.

"First," he began once Frost and O'Hara were seated across from him, "I want to thank you for agreeing to working with us under such unusual circumstances. I am aware of your prejudices, especially yours, Agent O'Hara, so I am honored all the more that you should choose to join me in the quest to save your countryman."

"I was not at liberty to discuss the pertinent details while we were still in Hong Kong, but now that we are well within my nation's air-space, I may speak freely. You," he nodded, indicating O'Hara, "were selected for this mission as the representative of the American Justice Department because of your outstanding career, through the years, in counter-terrorist work." His head tilted in Frost's direction. "You, Captain, were chosen for two reasons—your working relationship with Agent O'Hara which has proven so successful during your few encounters together and, of course, your own remarkable record as a mercenary. It was the unanimous decision of my superiors to go with you, Captain, our feeling being that if you weren't good at your chosen profession, you would not be alive."

"I appreciate the vote of confidence," the one-eyed man said.

"You should know, gentlemen, that the odds against us are great. The conference to initiate the mutual defense pact between our two nations was held outside Beijing near an ancient shrine west of the city. When the conference was attacked, only your American emissary, Bruce Thoresen, was spared and taken hostage. The Chinese representative, as well as the guards assigned to the conference, were all brutally murdered. One of the guards survived long enough to incriminate those responsible for the slaughter, but the poor man's internal injuries were beyond repair. He died several agonizing minutes after relaying his information."

"And who was it he fingered for the attack?" Frost asked.

Ling considered his answer, seeming to search his mind for the appropriate words, then replied. "They were devotees of the Night Ghosts, the Invisible Ones—Chinese equivalents of the more widely recognized Ninjas of Japan—those who have elevated the ways of death to an art form."

"And these Night Ghosts, their interest in kidnapping Thoresen . . ." Frost began.

"Was strictly financial," Ling continued, "an arrangement made with the pro-Soviet reactionary terrorists inside China—the same band of degenerates now holding emissary Thoresen prisoner. Official estimates are that within three, perhaps as many as four days, regardless of how valiantly Mr. Thoresen tries to resist, a full-disclosure statement concerning the purpose of his visit to China will be gotten from him. This disclosure could even take the form of a video tape with Thoresen reading it. Once he succumbs and gives them what they want, the terrorists will kill Thoresen and then smuggle his statement out of the country."

"Not if Frost and I have anything to say about it," O'Hara promised. "The first thing we do after we land in Peking, I want to take a ride out to where the conference took place, look around a bit, search the area, try and see if there might be something in the way of clues your people could have missed."

"We shall do precisely that," Ling confirmed. "A task force of crack Peking police and Social Affairs Department personnel has been assembled. Both of you are to be members of this task force, on equal footing with its commanders. For the time being we will forget that you are Americans; and you will forget that we are Communist Chinese. And who can say? Perhaps all of us will benefit from this marriage of convenience, unless the statement gets out and Mr. Thoresen is killed. If that happens . . ."

Frost grumbled, reaching for a cigarette. "We could all go up in smoke."

Chapter Six

The five car caravan threaded its way through the maze of traffic choking the streets of Peking, working a tenuous path across the city, heading for the highway leading to the Shrine of the Singing Tree—the site where the initial negotiations for the Sino-American defense pact had been conducted.

Met at the airport by a delegation of representatives from the special task force whose assignment it was to bring all matters concerning the Thorsen-abduction to a swift and successful close, Frost and O'Hara were officially greeted and welcomed by the People's Republic of China, then instructed to ride with Ling in the middle car of the caravan.

Wearing the Browning High Power in the Comvest shoulder holster under his jacket, plus the Gerber MkI boot knife in its sheath at the small of his back, Frost carried spare thirteen round magazines for the High Power on the off-gun side and in his pockets. All additional ammunition, along with the Interdynamics KG-99 assault pistol, were carried in the Safariland SWAT bag he often used as luggage.

Ling had explained as they were leaving the airport that, while automobiles were not as abundant as one would expect in a city of eight million, "Beijing still boasts more than two million bicycles."

"And right now it seems closer to three million," Frost thought to himself, the lack of proper rest the previous night, combined with the claustrophobic atmosphere of Peking's downtown area, putting an edge on his nerves which he found annoying. Everywhere he looked there were people—sheer masses of them—riding their bicycles, walking the streets, peddling their wares, eating their meals, caring for their young and old alike, going about the day-to-day struggle of getting by.

Trucks, cars, tractors, buses, pony carts, pedestrians and bicycles—all vying for a precious niche of vital space. From the back seat of the car he rode in Frost viewed numerous white-uniformed traffic police, positioned in elevated cabins at major intersections, barking orders into microphones that were totally ignored. It was the same with the traffic lights; of the scattered few Frost and the caravan encountered, it was quite evident from the chaos below in the streets that no one was paying the slightest bit of attention to them.

Finally, to Frost's relief, the caravan left the bulk of the city's traffic jams and crowded sidewalks behind, trading them instead for a winding road stretching across the countryside. Frost checked the time on his Rolex. It was now half past five in the afternoon. In the next couple of hours or so it would be dark. Long before nightfall, though—Ling had assured him—they would reach the Shrine of the Singing Tree. Once there, if they were lucky, either he or O'Hara could pick up a clue the others might have missed. Who could say? At any rate visiting the shrine was a good idea because that's where all the trouble had started in the first place. "Just like the Good Witch told Dorothy in Oz," Frost reflected. "It's always best to start at the beginning . . ."

The Shrine of the Singing Tree was about as unlikely a location for a murder and mayhem setting as Frost had seen. Protected on three sides by a series of low, tree covered hills, and facing at the front a quiet valley of chirping birds and buzzing insects, the shrine was a post card-perfect example of natural peace and harmony as the five car caravan pulled to a stop.

The first passenger out, Frost gingerly tested the air, expecting in part the same sulfurous mixture of fumes blanketing Peking to the east, but finding instead that the air was much cleaner here, delicately scented with sweet smelling blossoms. He stretched—his back aching from so much sitting—then waited for O'Hara and Ling to join him before walking together up the long flat steps climbing to the shrine.

According to Ling the shrine had been dedicated centuries earlier to commemorate the planting of a forest following a devastating blight which had destroyed most of the area's greenery. Since then, the Shrine of the Singing Tree had remained, through the years, a popular way station for travelers going to and from Peking. As such, Ling explained, the shrine had long enjoyed a reputation of constant beauty and serenity.

"So much for that reputation," O'Hara commented. "With all the stiffs popping up here lately, the shrine is sure to go down as one bad piece of real estate."

"Not at all, Agent O'Hara," Ling was quick to point out. "Simply because a great tragedy took place here is no reason to announce that fact to the general populace."

"Huh?" O'Hara frowned. "You mean they haven't been told?"

Ling shook his head. "To what purpose? Life is difficult enough without cluttering it unnecessarily."

"So nobody gets told," O'Hara said.

"That is correct. It would not be convenient."

Finding where the bodies had fallen during the massacre was easy. Everywhere Frost looked, from the stone walkway at the top of the steps which led to the shrine, to the interior of the ancient memorial itself—

the evidence of the savage attack was presented in abundance. Chalk marks, outlining where each victim had fallen, and with tags next to them designating the name of each victim in question, told Frost that more than twenty innocents had been sacrificed during Thoresen's kidnapping.

"The attack began here," Frost concluded, standing over a pair of outlines marked out near the top of the steps. "Notice how the feet of one victim faces the feet of the other? That tells us they were probably standing here, carrying on a conversation, when the double attack came, both being hit simultaneously." He knelt, carefully examing the closest outline, observing suspicious small pockets of reddish-brown staining the walkway where the victim's neck had been. A quick check confirmed the fact that there were similar stains around the opposite outline. "They were hit with garrotes first, slammed in their backs with a knee, and then dragged to the ground where their throats were cut. The poor guys probably saw each other going down, but by then there was nothing they could do about it. The killers left them bleeding to death, then moved on to their next target."

A single chalk-marked outline met them at the curve of the walkway, ten yards nearer to the shrine, O'Hara supplying the apparent details of the victim's demise. "He got it front and back, once with the garrote, then stabbed in the stomach. He was still alive when they left him, though, because the outline clearly shows how he was curled up into a ball, likely trying to hold his gut together, when he died. So far we're working with two highly efficient killers. They managed to get this far and bump off three guys without anyone sounding an alert." O'Hara shifted his gaze to Ling. "The man you mentioned, the one who survived long enough to finger the killers—was he able to tell you how many of these so-called Night Ghosts he saw?"

52

"He told the authorities he counted at least ten; the figure, though is difficult to judge since the man was delirious with pain at the time. We have estimated that the entire attack took under three minutes to complete, however, which would tend to support the man's story."

"Damn," O'Hara swore, "I was afraid you'd say that. If the two assassins out here could do so much damage, it scares me right down to my boxers to think what a whole pack of 'em could be capable of."

The story once they reached inside the shrine was much the same—outlines of bodies and, in two cases, parts of bodies, strewn across the floor.

"What's the word on this one?" Frost asked, standing over an outline which ended at the shoulders.

"That was Zhu Guodeng, representative of the People's Republic for the negotiations," Ling explained, his normally placid face suddenly registering what Frost saw was sadness. "Zhu was a good man. He was my friend. I knew him well. He did not deserve such butchery. Those who murdered him cut off his head, taking it with them. Zhu Guodeng deserved better."

"I'm sorry, Ling," Frost told him. "I know how you feel. There was a time when I lost friends, many of them, but just like I got even for their deaths, we'll get even for Zhu Guodeng."*

"Thank you, Captain Frost." Ling sighed to himself, regaining much of his lost composure. "I believe what you are telling me and accept it as fact. When the time comes, as it must, my friend's death will be avenged."

Further investigation of the scene of the crime produced no startling revelations of physical evidence, Frost noted bitterly. As was true with most homicide investigations, all obvious evidential material on or near each body had been processed before the body in question was removed for medical examination. Beyond

*See, THEY CALL ME THE MERCENARY #1, *The Killer Genesis*

establishing the cause of each death, though, the investigators had found little else to work with, and subsequent searching of the crime site for less obvious trace evidence had added nothing of value to their findings.

Movement to his right caught Frost's attention as a plainclothes policeman entered the shrine, quickly seeking out Ling Wao. The two men exchanged information in a blinding series of Chinese sentences, then Ling dismissed and thanked him by saying "shay-shay," turning to Frost and O'Hara as the man departed.

"It is good news," he said. "Component members of our special task force have located what may well be a training facility for the cursed Invisible Ones—the Night Ghosts."

"Great!" O'Hara smacked the palm of his left hand with his right fist. "Now, we're gettin' somewhere. Whatta ya say we bust in on 'em and pay them a visit? Even if Thoresen isn't there we still might be able to take one of those creeps alive. And one of your guys," and O'Hara turned to Ling, "could get him to talk."

"We do have our tutors," Ling agreed. "Whether or not we shall have use for them remains to be seen." He looked at his watch. "We will not be taking the caravan back into Peking. A helicopter will be arriving outside the shrine to pick us up in five minutes. From here we will fly to a location near the suspected Night Ghosts' training facility, there to join the remaining members of our team and conduct a raid on the suspected camp. Are there any questions?"

Chapter Seven

Sunset was still more than an hour away as the entire special task force team met to discuss the plan of penetrating the suspected Night Ghost training facility. Flown from the Shrine of the Singing Tree in a Whirlwind-25—a Chinese copy of the large Soviet Mi-4 helicopter—Frost and O'Hara were waiting for Ling to call the meeting to order when O'Hara excitedly pulled Frost to the side.

"What's up?" the one-eyed man asked.

"Plenty. Do you see that woman over there, the one standing talking to Ling?"

Frost looked to where O'Hara indicated. Talking to the S.A.D. agent who had served as their escort from Hong Kong was a Chinese woman in her late 20s. She appeared tall to Frost—at least three inches taller than Ling—had straight black hair worn long over her shoulders, and possessed a lovely face that belonged on a movie screen. Frost decided she was beautiful.

"Yeah, I see her, Mike. Who is she?"

"Her name is Elizabeth Chu'an. Back home the Bureau's got a file on her this thick." He showed Frost a wide space between the thumb and forefinger of his right hand. "In the upper echelon of the Communist Chinese Secret Service, she's damn near right at the top."

"That must make her pretty good."

"One of the best. On at least two separate occasions

that I know of she entered the U.S. illegally for the purpose of carrying out high level espionage assignments. In each case, by the time we caught wind of her act, she had slipped safely out of the country. The closest we came to nailing her came two years ago at Los Angeles International Airport. One of our agents got a positive make on her out in one of the parking lots, then made the mistake of trying to bring her in alone."

"But she escaped," Frost guessed.

"After cracking four of the agent's ribs and breaking his jaw in two places, yeah, you could say that she got away, all right. And here she is now not twenty feet from us and I can't even touch her."

"It might be dangerous if you tried to, Mike. Besides, if she is as good as you say, her experience could really prove useful."

"I guess so," O'Hara said. "But you know what? After this gig is finished I wouldn't mind inviting her to fly with me on a one-way ticket to Washington. You think she'd go for it?"

"Beats me, O'Hara. Why not ask her yourself. Ling's bringing her over to meet us right now."

"The rat," O'Hara commented. "That's just like him ..."

"Gentlemen," Ling announced, the tall, dark-haired beauty by his side. "It is my honor and pleasure to introduce to you ..."

"Elizabeth Chu'an," O'Hara supplied. "I know all about her, Ling. Miss Chu'an and I almost had the privilege of meeting—on an official basis back in the States. Unfortunately, she changed her time schedule and the blessed event never took place."

"You must be Mike O'Hara," the woman smiled, sounding more American to Frost than some Americans he knew. "I apologize for not meeting you earlier, but professional commitments being what they were, such a meeting would have been impossible. And anyway, I'm sure you know how hard it is to catch an international flight at L.A.X. I am pleased to correct that oversight and to meet you now."

The woman extended her hand to O'Hara, which Frost's friend from the FBI reluctantly shook.

"It is good that you would shake my hand," Elizabeth Chu'an said, breaking the handshake. "The ability to overlook your prejudices is a difficult task to master. In 1954, at the first Geneva conference on Indochina, when your American Secretary of State, John Foster Dulles, refused to shake hands with Zhou Enlai, he was not mastering his prejudices. I am pleased, Agent O'Hara, that you elected not to repeat that diplomatic snub."

O'Hara, open-mouthed, could think of nothing to say as Ling carried on with the introduction. "And this, Miss Chu'an, is Captain Hank Frost, the second man chosen by the Americans to accompany us on our mission."

Without waiting, Frost thrust his hand out for the woman—obviously pleased and somewhat amused by the speed at which the hand had appeared—which she gratefully accepted.

"Mike's told me all about you, Miss Chu'an . . ."

"Please, Captain. I prefer Elizabeth."

"Okay. Anyway, like I was saying, Mike's told me all about you. If even half of it's true it will be reassuring to know that you're able to take care of yourself when the need arises."

"I am not one to be babied, if that's what you mean." She glanced over to Ling. "It is growing late. I suggest we discuss our plans, then get underway. If we must engage in conflict with the Invisible Ones, it will be bad enough to do so while it is still light out, much more dangerous once it is dark. Shall we?"

The plan was one of simplicity. Rather than opt for a

full scale attack using the entire task force—Frost counted more than thirty people gathered altogether—it was decided that sending in a smaller advance party of eight would better suit their purposes. Fewer people could move faster and quieter than a larger group, and so were more likely to reach the area of the suspected insurgent's camp undetected. In the event that the remaining members of the task force were needed, they could be contacted via a radio signal and airlifted in aboard one of the two Whirlwind-25 helicopters that were parked in a nearby field.

Once the basic plan was agreed to, Ling called out the names of those who would accompany him on the attack. Frost, O'Hara, and the woman, Elizabeth Chu'an, were singled out, plus four others—three men and another woman. After that Ling dismissed the balance of the task force, then gave those who would be going with him ten minutes to secure their gear before setting out.

O'Hara eased the Model 60 Smith & Wesson back into the Cobra Hugger ankle holster on his left ankle, reseated the reinforced thumb snap release, then nodded to Frost. "That's me all packed for the party. Anyway you cut it I'm ready for bear. How about you?"

"Almost." Frost opened his Safariland SWAT bag and removed the Interdynamics KG-99 assault pistol, with sling and flash suppressor in place, fully loaded with a thirty-six round magazine up its well. He moved the KG-99's sling onto his left shoulder over his head, keeping the weapon cross body beneath his right arm, then reached back into the bag for two spare magazines, which he slipped into his belt. He rezipped the SWAT bag closed and then, satisfied that he was ready, reported to O'Hara, "That's all she wrote, 'Ace.' Let's go."

Together they crossed to where Ling and the others were waiting, Frost noting as they did that both Ling and Elizabeth Chu'an were now outfitted with K-50M submachineguns, Chinese versions of the Russian PPS-41, each weighing 9.5 pounds and equipped with a 7.62mm thirty-five-round magazine. The remaining four members of the group carried the same Type 56 assault rifle that Frost had used during the battle on the *Fast Fish.*

Ling ran a final check to make sure nothing they might need had been overlooked then, on his command—and with Ling's quick steps setting the pace—they were off. Within minutes after their departure the narrow trail they were following rounded an outcropping of rock, leaving the balance of the task force behind them and out of sight. Gradually, after a hundred yards, the trail took a rising sharp turn to the right and they began to climb.

"How far up and back will we be going?" Frost asked, already aware of the subtle change in air temperature and regretting there'd been no time to change to more appropriate clothes for the field. Down in the valley where they had started, the early evening air had been sticky, heavy with moisture. But now, with each new step taking them that much higher into the mountains, it was decidedly cooler.

"The site of the Night Ghosts' training facility is located in the ruins of a Lung-men temple," Ling explained, his rapid stepping pace showing no signs of letting up. "The shrine is patterned after those to be found along the high river bank south of the city of Lo-yang in Honan Province, and was most likely constructed at some time between the end of the fifth and the beginning of the eighth centuries."

"That old, huh?" O'Hara spoke up. "And it's still standing?"

Ling's response was immediate. "We are not speaking of modern architecture's obsession with obsolescence as you know it, Agent O'Hara—the kind you see in America where a corner gasoline service station is torn down so that another one exactly like it can be built in its place. No, when the ancient temples and shrines were constructed in China they were meant to last an eternity and, while some deterioration has predictably occurred over the centuries since the temple we are going to was first erected, the original flavor and mastery of its architects will still be very much in evidence."

"So some of it's still standing," O'Hara said. "That's all I asked."

"You are welcome, Agent O'Hara," Ling chuckled, visibly pleased with his impromptu defense of Chinese architecture, then spoke to Frost. "As to your question, Captain, of how far we must journey to reach our destination, my guess would be more than a mile, but less than two."

"Great," the one-eyed man said, stepping over a log which had fallen across the trail. "Spoken like a diplomat. When we landed in the helicopters back in the valley—any chance that they heard us fly in?"

"It is possible," Ling considered, "but I think not. The mountains and hills have a habit of remaining silent even during a storm."

"Whether we were heard or not makes no difference." Elizabeth Chu'an increased her pace so that she was walking beside Frost. "The Night Ghosts will be expecting us."

Frost squinted at her with his right eye. "Why should that be?"

"It is their way, Hank Frost," she replied. "The Invisible Ones put the word 'art' into the Art of Killing. As such, they live with death constantly. They will expect us because we mean to kill them, and they are always expecting to die."

"Unless they succeed in killing us first," Ling added.

"Yin and Yang," Elizabeth Chu'an nodded. "There is that possibility too."

"Some pep talk," Frost grumbled. "I'm sorry I asked."

Chapter Eight

The one-eyed man had never seen anything to match his first glimpse of the ancient Lung-men temple. China seemed to him a land of surprise in its infinite beauty. Like an elaborate movie set for a cinematic triumph, the vista presented to him was, he felt, at once both awe-inspiring and mysterious.

"Magnificent," he whispered, his eye taking in a view few westerners had witnessed. Perched atop a tree-lined ridge overlooking the temple site, the trail they had followed had come to an abrupt end, culminating in a steep staircase cut from the living rock of the mountain. Frost estimated the staircase, its bottom-most steps lost in a canopy of tree branches and vines, descended for more than two hundred feet before opening up at the gateway to the temple.

From his vantage point on the ridge above, Frost had no difficulty seeing over the wall surrounding the temple and beyond. Hidden in a canyon of sheer walls and jagged peaks, the temple proper stretched across the floor of the canyon as far as the eye could see, there to disappear from sight around a great outcropping of stone. Innumerable statues of Buddha, each wearing varying expressions of temperament, towered over the canyon's floor—many of the statues reaching as high as seventy feet into the air. It was not their impressive size, though, that Frost found to be the statues' most marvelous aspect, but the obvious fact that each of the statues had been sculpted and carved from the wall of the canyon itself.

"I'd always heard the Chinese were good chiselers," he commented softly to O'Hara.

Initially, Frost had thought the temple deserted, but now as he watched, a single column of black-clad figures suddenly appeared—Night Ghosts! Running in formation, weaving a path in and about the maze of Buddha statues, their arms and legs flowing from one side to the other in a synchronized wave of motion. The Invisible Ones moved as a single unit across the sandy canyon floor, their passage failing to raise the slightest cloud of dust.

"How can they all run around like that and not kick up some dirt?" O'Hara asked the question, and Elizabeth Chu'an replied.

"It is said of the Night Ghosts that they walk the earth without touching the earth; that they may cross a field of grass and not disturb a solitary blade."

Seeing them now, the Night Ghosts going through their choreographed moves, Frost could almost believe it. Quickly, he counted the number of runners below, coming up with a total—fifteen—five more than those suspected of participating in the raid and massacre at the Shrine of the Singing Tree. A few of the Invisible Ones had apparently been left behind to watch the fort during the attack.

"Whatta ya think, Frost?" O'Hara leaned over to the one-eyed man. "Fifteen of them to eight of us. That shouldn't be such a big . . . Awww, shit!"

Frost saw them the same time O'Hara did—a second column of Night Ghosts—again fifteen in number, dashing swiftly around from the base of a particularly large statue, moving on a break-neck collision course with the head of the first column. But the collision never happened as the lead figure of each column turned to his right at the last possible second, never slowing down, only to double back to the left a heartbeat later, diving in and out with precise movements between one and another, the two columns becoming one, and then becoming two again.

"Not bad," Frost observed, trying not to sound too impressed. "If they could do that stunt for the half-time show at the next Army-Navy game, it would win 'em an Emmy for sure. Now Mike, what were you saying about odds?"

"They're up to close to four-to-one now, and that's just counting the birds we can see. There's no telling how many more of 'em there are. Maybe now would be as good a time as any to radio in for the rest of the troops?"

"That's too dangerous," Frost disagreed with his friend. "We're not one hundred percent positive that Bruce Thoresen isn't being held captive somewhere in the temple. If he is down there and we go calling for the choppers to come flying in, one of the first things those Night Ghost crazies are gonna do is give Thoresen the ax."

"Yeah, I know, Frost," O'Hara told him. "But now that I have a better idea of what we're up against, I'm not so sure we can handle it on our own."

"What, are you kidding, Mike? Of course we can handle it. Haven't you ever heard that 'Eight is Enough?'" Frost chuckled alone at that one, then said seriously to his pal from the FBI, "Tell ya what—if it gets too hot for us in the temple, then you've got my word that we just turn around and march right back up here to the ridge and wait for help. How's that sound?"

O'Hara grunted, "Like bullshit sunnyside-up. Let's get it over with, then. The suspense is killing me . . ."

They made it from the ridge to the bottom of the great stone stairway unchallenged, emerging from the

64

descent onto a smoothed-by-time brick path which led, after rounding a curve, to the temple's entrance. On the way down the steep decline Frost had functioned the KG-99, found the bolt with his left hand, slowly drawn it back, then eased it forward, closing the bolt and stripping out the top round in the magazine. O'Hara was equally prepared, the big .44 Magnum he always carried wrapped tightly in his fist, the look on his face one of pure determination.

Wordlessly, weapons ready, they left the shelter and security of the tree-covered stairway, hurrying along the brick path, the final minutes of daylight casting shimmering patterns of brilliant reds and yellows against the backdrop of the canyon walls. They rounded the curve in the path then and Frost licked his lips, swallowing hard. If there had been any question as to whether or not the Night Ghosts had indeed been responsible for the atrocities at the Shrine of the Singing Tree, all doubts were erased forever by the horrible sight confronting Frost and the others: a human head staked to the end of a short iron spike, its eyeless sockets less than two feet from the ground.

"Zhu Guodeng?" Frost turned to Ling, but no answer was necessary. The overwhelming sadness washing across Ling's face confirmed the head's identity.

A solitary tear trickled down Ling's cheek, Frost judging the respect Ling felt for his departed friend's memory not permitting him to wipe the tear away. Instead, his expression of sorrow was replaced by one of anger and contempt.

"Remember your promise, Captain."

"I will," Frost said. "You can ..."

There was a whooshing noise ending with a wet-sounding smack, and the man standing next to Frost toppled backward to the ground—dead with an eight-pointed heavy weight shuriken throwing star buried in his forehead. Frost spun toward the temple gateway, ready to begin blazing away with the KG-99 assault pistol, but there was nothing to shoot at.

"What the hell?" the one-eyed man swore to himself as the dry rattle of laughter came at them from the opposite side of the wall beyond the gateway. Then, as suddenly as it had started, the laughter stopped, to be replaced instead by the black-clad image of a lone Night Ghost warrior who casually appeared, arms hanging loosely at his side, walking to the center of the temple's entrance, blocking their way.

The man, his face concealed so that only his dark eyes were visible, hissed out a stream of angry words.

"He says that we are trespassing on hallowed land," Ling translated, "and that, unless we depart immediately, all of us are doomed to die."

O'Hara, his Model 29 trained on the Night Ghost's chest, spoke without taking his eyes from his target. "Say the word, Ling, and I blow the sucker into the next province."

"That won't be necessary." Ling signalled to another member of the task force by name. "Huang!"

Automatically, the man called Huang responded to Ling's implied command, dropping his Type-56 assault rifle to the ground, then boldly advancing to stand in front of the Night Ghost—hands on his hips, words Frost interpreted as taunting in nature springing from his lips.

"What's going on?" Frost asked Elizabeth Chu'an as the woman came slowly up to be by his side.

"Huang has called the Night Ghost a braggart and a swine, but chiefly a coward and a weakling for hiding behind weapons of steel. Huang has challenged the Night Ghost to defend the honor of his order by meeting him in combat, face-to-face, unarmed."

The Night Ghost stood motionless, not saying a word.

"Will he go for it, Elizabeth?"

"It is difficult to gauge the Night Ghost's response. He knows we are reluctant to fire upon him for fear of alerting his comrades. At the same time he cannot call for help because to do so would be a disgrace. Once his friends had come to his aid, they would be duty-bound to slay him afterward, thereby keeping the pride of the order intact."

"Nice," Frost said, then the Night Ghost muttered something foul-sounding under his breath and opened his fists—the action depositing two more of the star-shaped shuriken to the canyon's dirt floor. "I think we've got a fight."

"Huang has shamed the Night Ghost into meeting his challenge," the woman confirmed. "They will fight."

With Frost and the others watching, Huang and the black-clad assassin squared off, each adopting a distinctive martial arts stance.

"It is chuan fa," Elizabeth told him. "What you would know as kung-fu."

Then, while the woman provided a technical commentary of the chaun fa contest, the challengers began their bout.

The Night Ghost stood with his legs braced apart, right leg straight, knee of the left leg slightly bent, most of his weight on the forward right leg. His hands were clenched into double fists, the right drawn in close to his chest, his left fully extended—his openly hostile attitude and overall stance branding him to Frost as a practitioner of hard-style kung fu.

Huang's style was of the internal or soft form—his legs braced evenly apart, both knees bent, his arms extended with the palms of his hands turned up. His was a pliable stance, one of apparent relaxed defense.

Shifting suddenly on his feet the Night Ghost

attacked, leaping forward out of his basic front stance, right fist driving out in a thumb-knuckle strike for Huang's solar plexus. But the blow never landed as Huang retaliated with a perfectly timed palm-heel block, flying in front of his body, deflecting the Night Ghost's punch out and away, then quickly following up the block with a well-executed palm-heel strike that struck the stunned Night Ghost hard in the face.

The black-clad fanatic stumbled back in surprise, made a growling noise deep in his throat, and attacked again, fist and forearm working together in a classic hammer-fist strike. Huang deflected the blow off to the side, then swept both arms in a circular motion, out and then in, striking with a wide variation of the popular U punch—both hands hitting his opponent in a simultaneous blur—one curved fist smashing to the Night Ghost's nose, the other cutting a path of destruction across the assassin's midsection. Before the man could recover, Huang swept his right leg out in a swinging kick that caught the Night Ghost directly behind the knees, throwing him to the ground with a thud. He moaned and tried to rise to his feet, but a furious knife hand blow delivered by Huang to the center of the doomed man's throat brought his career as an Invisible One to a swift and final conclusion.

Huang, barely winded from the exercise, backed away from the body of the Night Ghost, a broad smile on his face.

"Way to go!" O'Hara grinned.

"Yeah, but it's only Round One," Frost said, looking through the gateway and into the temple. "And if my eye isn't playing tricks on me—here comes Round Two right now!"

"Damn!" O'Hara swore as the two columns of Night Ghosts, thirty killers in all, came charging around one of

68

the giant Buddha statues a hundred yards away, weapons held high, running straight at them. "Double-damn!"

Frost rasped. "You've got my vote on that one!"

Chapter Nine

Frost met the Night Ghosts' attack head on, charging through the gateway onto the temple grounds, the first finger of his right hand working the KG-99's trigger, the assault pistol belching a series of two-round semi-automatic bursts into the nearest of his foes. Fifty yards and closing the first of the 115-grain semi-jacketted hollow points struck home—the JHPs cutting across the lead man of each column, bringing them down—one killer dying as most of his face took an unexpected vacation, the other Night Ghost buying it with a two-round burst of gliding metal jacketted lead to the heart, flopping him to the ground like a bad sack of garbage.

The loud booming of O'Hara's .44 Magnum split the canyon like thunder as two more of the Night Ghosts tumbled to the dirt—the 180-grain JHPs O'Hara favored lifting one of the targets completely off his twitching feet, while a follow-up blast bowled another assassin over with a solid hit to the gut.

Frost ran, finger still pumping the KG-99's trigger, as the rest of the task force team opened fire, too, the sharp crackling of Elizabeth's K-50M SMG pounding three Night Ghosts to death with a trio of headshots. Behind them, another pair of killers went down—the first thanks to a nice shot by Huang that caught the soon-to-be-dead Night Ghost in the side of his neck, severing the jugular so that blood spurted everywhere; the second assassin perishing when a triple dash of death from Ling's Sino-copy of the Russian PPS-41 delivered 7.62mms fast and hard.

Nine of the Night Ghosts were history, Frost thought—ten counting the man back at the gate. But the determined black-clad terrorists were still coming at them, refusing to break formation. Frost fired his KG-99 empty, running and reaching the corner of one of the Buddha statues, stripping the spent magazine from the KG-99, loading one of the thirty-six-round spares in its place, yanking back on the bolt.

"Frost!"

O'Hara's voice, a warning. The one-eyed man wheeled, turning instinctively as the thirty-inch single edged blade of the Cern Do, double broadsword, came at him, whistling through the air in an attempt to separate Frost's head from his shoulders. Frost dropped low, the Cern Do's razor-sharp blade brushing above his hairline, missing him, crashing with a jarring clang against the massive legs of the Buddha statue.

The Night Ghost recovered, swept his arm up high and back, eager to chop Frost in two. The KG-99, Frost twisting the gun in his hand, jamming the auto pistol's muzzle deep into the Night Ghost's unprotected stomach. Firing, the sword starting down, three sets of two-round bursts popping the man's belly open like an overripe melon. Whimpering sounds, animal-like, inhuman, the sword falling from dead fingers as Frost pushed away, the pointed end of the Cern Do stabbing into the ground near his thigh.

The one-eyed man jumped to his feet, shadows of danger moving out of the corner of his right eye, wheeling then, spinning in place, seeing them—two of the Night Ghosts and no time to fire—grabbing at the curved Cern Do handle, pulling it free in an upward slash, spearing the first of his enemies through the chest, the blade lodged there, torn from his grasp.

Frost shifted to his side as the second assassin leaped, striking him, spilling them both to the ground in a flurry of punches and jabs. A vicious backhand caught Frost on the chin, red and green floaters dancing across his eye as he felt the statue of stone pressed at his back—the KG-99 out of reach and useless, wedged between him and the Buddha.

The Night Ghost dove in for the kill, hands clutching at Frost's throat, the mask of material covering the assassin's mouth torn away, the killer leaning down, pressing his face above Frost's, foul breath, gritting teeth—and something else.

Frost fought, turning his head, hearing the sound as the deadly needle came spitting from the Night Ghost's mouth, aimed at his right eye, but lodging instead in the patch of black cloth where his left eye had been.

"Sorry, sucker," Frost managed, despite the fact that he was being choked to death. "Somebody already beat you to it."

Screaming in anger because the man trying to kill him had also tried blinding him in his good eye, Frost shook his body like a madman, bringing his hands up between those clamped to his throat, separating them, breaking the stranglehold, then hammering his would-be killer's face with the knife edges of his hands. The man was moaning loudly, blood gushing from his broken nose, as Frost wriggled free from under him, snatching the KG-99 around on its sling.

"Chokes me up to have to do this," Frost grinned, then killed the Night Ghost instantly with a quick two-shot burst to the head. Gingerly, using the thumb and forefinger of his left hand, Frost removed the needle embedded in his eyepatch, letting it fall.

The sounds of death were everywhere as Frost came out from behind the Buddha statue, the KG-99 jumping slightly in his hands as he took down another Cern Do-wielding crazy—this one preparing to nail an unsuspecting Ling. Once, twice, three times his fingers flexed on the trigger, grinding the swordsman down, the line of gilding metal-jacketed hollow points doing their work.

"Shay-shay," Ling shouted his thanks, swinging his K-50M SMG into the path of an oncoming Night Ghost, blasting the killer.

Satisfied that Ling was holding his own, Frost turned and ran, further up the canyon, weaving in and out of the temple's statues, rounding one of the larger monuments in time to see O'Hara pull the plug on a Night Ghost trying to cut him down with a kusarigama—a short scythe attached to a long chain with a weight at its end; the weight was a spiked metal ball. As the one-eyed man watched, O'Hara's Model 29 boomed out twice, stopping the Night Ghost in his tabi boots, and sending the blade of the out-of-control kusarigama flying over the canyon floor, straight into the disbelieving mouth of another assassin.

Three more Night Ghosts were moving into position around O'Hara, each seeming to Frost to be in a race to see who could bag the lanky FBI agent first. Two of the assassins were rushing O'Hara from opposite sides, both wildly swinging kusarigama scythe weapons over their heads. The third killer was armed with the deadly shuriken throwing stars.

O'Hara wheeled, firing at and hitting the shuriken-throwing figure in black, the .44 Magnum striking his chest and hammering him down, but not before the killer had unleashed two of his star-shaped blades, one of which struck O'Hara and stayed in the tender deltoid muscle area of his right shoulder. O'Hara screamed as the shuriken bit into his flesh, his left hand reaching over to pull the death star out, the Model 29 sailing from his fingers.

73

And the kusarigama killers were nearly upon him.

Frost twisted to his left, aiming with the KG-99 assault pistol, pulling the trigger, a three-round semi-automatic burst of the 115-grain JHPs pumping into the target, bringing him down. Turning to the right, zeroing in on the final attacker, pulling the trigger of the KG-99, then nothing—the magazine coming up dry. No time to reload, Frost let the KG-99 drop, flashing his right hand under his jacket, seeing O'Hara fumbling through his pain for the .38 Chiefs stuffed in his ankle holster, moving too slow, Frost's right hand coming away from the jacket, right thumb jacking back the hammer of the Metalifed Browning High Power, the first finger of his right hand snapping inside the trigger guard as the muzzle came up, pumping once and then twice, both shots going to the Night Ghost's center of mass.

The dead assassin was still completing his fall to the ground when Frost ran over to O'Hara.

"That was a close one, Mike."

"Tell me something I don't know, Frost." O'Hara stood, the bloody results of his wounded shoulder soaking through his coat. "And yes, it hurts like hell in case you were wondering!"

"I'll take your word for it." He picked up his friend's Model 29 from the dirt where it had dropped, then brought it back and handed it to O'Hara. "You want me to reload it for you?"

"I can manage, thanks."

Frost glanced from side to side. The canyon was swirling in shadows now, purple fingers of night coming to claim the temple. Bodies of the Night Ghosts were everywhere, sprawled in assorted poses of death; and there was the sound of sporadic gunfire—one of the K-50M SMGs by the sharp cracking noise—but no one else from the task force was visible.

"What's the score, O'Hara?"

74

"Jeez." The FBI man finished reloading his big .44 with a fresh supply of 180-grain JHPs from a Safariland speedloader. "Huang caught it with one of those funny-lookin' swords, right after I shouted to you. Then we lost the woman . . ."

"Not . . .?" Frost began.

"Nah, not Elizabeth Chu'an. She's okay. I mean the other woman. She got hit hard with a knife-chain gizzmo—like the ones that almost got me."

"The kusarigamas," Frost told him.

"Yeah, well whatever the hell it was, it killed her clean as a whistle."

"What about the Night Ghosts?"

"All of 'em dead as far as I know, but . . ."

"Wait, O'Hara—do you smell it?"

"Whatta ya talking about . . . yeah, now I do."

"Smoke!" Frost practically shouted. "Come on!"

"God, Frost—you don't think they're tryin' to cook Thoresen?"

But as they rounded the canyon's great outcropping of stone there was no sight of the kidnapped American; only a single Night Ghost who was dumping a container of papers onto the flames of a roaring bonfire.

"Stop him, Frost!"

At the sound of O'Hara's voice the Night Ghost spun on his heels, a shuriken throwing star clenched in his fist, ready to throw, Frost's Browning High Power flipping him off his feet and onto the blazing flames.

Trying hard to ignore the tremendous heat from the bonfire, Frost grabbed the end of a burning branch, digging through the flames, desperately trying to salvage any of the papers the Night Ghost had attempted to destroy—the results—other than loss of the hair on his right hand—the recovery of a solitary piece of paper, badly burned on all four sides.

"That's it?" O'Hara asked as Frost pulled his prize

away from the flames. "One lousy piece of paper?"

"That's all," Frost reported. "The rest got roasted."

"So whatta we do now?"

"Find Ling and have him radio for a chopper to fly us out."

"Hmm, that sounds familiar. I made that same suggestion earlier."

"I know you did. But it seemed like a bad idea at the time."

"And a good idea now?"

"Yeah," Frost answered. "A damn good idea."

Chapter Ten

It took seven stitches and one tetanus shot to put O'Hara shoulder back together again, yet when Frost's lanky friend emerged from the doctor's office into the waiting room, he was all smiles.

"Why all the teeth, O'Hara? When you went in you were moaning like the doc was going to have to put you to sleep. What gives?"

"Nothing, Frost. I feel good. In fact, I never felt better in my life."

Frost shook his head. "Something's fishy. What'd the doc do—feed you a happy pill?"

"Uh uh." O'Hara replied, slipping back into his coat. "But before he started sewing me up he jabbed me all over my back and shoulder with a bunch of these little needles. It was magic, Frost. I didn't feel any pain at all, not a bit."

"Congratulations," Frost said. "Now, you wanna go? The party's about to begin." It was a "party" Frost didn't want to miss.

All during the ride from the doctor's office to the building housing the main headquarters for the Peking Police Department, O'Hara talked nonstop about his "absolutely fantastic" acupuncture treatment. Finally, inside the building and heading upstairs for the crime lab on the second floor, Frost—feeling frustrated—threw his hands in the air in mock surrender.

"All right, all right. Enough, O'Hara. You win. I'm convinced. And as soon as we're finished at the crime lab I'm gonna volunteer to have someone zap me with one of those flying stars just like what happened to you. Maybe then, after I've had the stitches and the shot and all the little needles, it'll be easier for me to get with the program."

"Gee, Frost," O'Hara worked his lips into a pout. "You should've said something if I was gettin' on your nerves. You won't hear me mention another word about the acupuncture. Honest."

"Great. It's a deal."

They were greeted at the entrance to the crime lab by Ling Wao.

"You are in time, gentlemen," he informed them. "The report on the piece of paper which was rescued following our battle at the temple has not been released yet."

"Good," Frost said. "At least we haven't missed anything."

"Not a problem," Ling assured Frost. "We should have at least ten minutes to ourselves." Then he shifted his attention to O'Hara. "So, Mike—how is the shoulder?"

Frost rolled his eye to the ceiling and went to find Elizabeth Chu'an.

Fifteen minutes later the decoded contents of the document Frost had seized were revealed to mixed reviews. On the one hand the document proved that kidnapped American Emissary, Bruce Thoresen, was still alive. The bad news part came with the discovery of where Thoresen had been taken.

"We have pinpointed the probable location where Emissary Thoresen is being held," Ling said, reading from the lab report. "From information contained in the captured document we know that Mr. Thoresen is being held prisoner deep within China in an isolated section of Sichuan province, part of the Yangtze river country."

"How isolated an area are you talking about?" Frost asked.

"Not so out of the way that we couldn't fly in on top of them, but we all know the ramifications of such a move. Emissary Thoresen would be executed before the first of our people could rappel from the helicopter to the ground."

"Okay, so dropping us in is out of the question." The one-eyed man fed the end of a Camel into the blue-yellow flame of his battered Zippo. "What about alternatives? There has to be another way in."

"There is, Captain Frost. And while precious time will be lost by our utilizing this alternative route, doing so will reduce the prospect of alerting the kidnappers to our presence."

Frost shifted his body weight from one foot to the other. "When do we leave?"

"We will be allowed to change clothes and to clean up, after which we are scheduled to depart at 0100 hours."

"And don't tell me," Frost held up his hand, "we're flying out of town on our old friend, the Mayo-Gwantsi—the pride of No Sweat Airways."

"Very good," Ling grinned. "You are catching on, I believe the expression is."

"Slowly but surely," Frost agreed.

Which was when the bomb went off—rocking the floor, shattering windows, driving long wide cracks up the walls. Their ears were still ringing from the explosion when, from somewhere below on the first floor of the building, the unmistakable chatter of gunfire could be heard.

"What the . . . ?" O'Hara began.

"Those dirty sons-of- . . ." Frost picked up where O'Hara left off. "We're under attack!"

There was a scream, immediately followed by another explosion, much louder than the first, rocking the floor beneath their feet again and sending great portions of the ceiling crashing down. A female lab assistant stumbled in from the hallway, crying hysterically, her bloody fingers desperately tugging at an eight-inch shard of window glass lodged in her thigh. As Elizabeth hurried over to try and save the woman's life, Frost—drawing his Browning High Power and thumbing back the hammer—started running into the corridor. "Come on!"

"Those bastards have to be crazy to pull a stunt like this," O'Hara said, the six-inch Smith & Wesson Model 29 coming into his fist. "We're in the damn Peking Police Headquarters for cryin' out loud!"

"So tell them that!" Frost advised. "Maybe they're hitting the wrong place and don't know it," he rasped.

They were rushing together along the hallway, making for the stairwell leading downstairs.

"You can be sure the enemy is well aware of its target," Ling said in a hurry, the Chinese Type 51 Tokarev pistol appearing in his right hand. "The Night Ghosts are disgraced by their defeat at our hands at the Lung-men temple. For so many to lose to so few is a great burden of shame. They are attacking now to reclaim their pride."

"But I thought we smoked 'em all out at the temple?" O'Hara complained, bumping into Frost as they ran.

"We did," Ling confirmed. "But those who perished were but a small faction of the entire Night Ghost membership."

"Terrific," O'Hara grumbled, absently rubbing the stitched-up wound in his shoulder.

"What are you worried about, O'Hara?" Frost joked. "If you get nabbed again, we'll just pop you back to that doc friend of yours and have him patch you up with some more little needles."

"Ha, ha!" O'Hara wasn't laughing.

"Aaaiiieeeee!" the cry came from the right as one of the office doors suddenly burst open, a shrieking Night Ghost—the middle finger of each hand inserted into the handle-holes of a ring knife—running, charging toward them.

Frost and O'Hara reacted to the attack, each firing once with his weapon; Frost's Browning catching the man low in the gut, while O'Hara's .44 Magnum blew away most of the killer's right knee, O'Hara shouting, "Jeez—my shoulder!"

But a second killer, armed like the first, was coming.

Frost saw Ling as the S.A.D. agent jumped fearlessly into the line of attack, seemingly oblivious of the double-edged ring knives about to slash him across the face, as he raised his Type 51 Tokarev pistol and fired—two shots—both of the 7.62mm slugs crashing into the Night Ghost's forehead and bringing him down.

"What the hell?" O'Hara stammered.

"He was using opium," Ling said curtly.

"Go for the head, O'Hara," Frost told his friend. "If they're so hopped up, headshots are what we'll have to use."

"Right."

Three headshots and three dead Night Ghosts later they reached the top of the stairs and started down, stepping as they did, over the throat-slashed bodies of two Peking PD officers. Taking the steps as fast as he dared, Frost reached the first floor ahead of O'Hara and

Ling, bursting into the corridor, instinct forcing him to drop to the floor and roll to the left as assault rifle shots hammered into the wall.

Frost came out of the roll with a stream of bullets chewing up the floor tiles near his head. Something tugged hard at the fabric of his jacket's right sleeve, then he caught sight of the man with the rifle and opened up with the High Power—pounding a trio of JHPs into the chest of the fanatical commando. The corpse was half-way on its tumble to the floor when a second assailant appeared to take its place, but Frost heard the boom from O'Hara's Smith and Wesson. "Gotta shoot left-handed—Jeez!"

"The Night Ghosts are not alone in this madness," Ling commented to Frost as he joined the one-eyed man and O'Hara. "Some of the pro-Soviet reactionaries behind the kidnapping of Emissary Thoresen are here assisting the Invisible Ones."

"That's how I figured it." Frost climbed to his feet. "But what they're doing is suicide. For the Night Ghosts the attack is a matter of saving face, but for the pro-Soviet terrs ... ?"

"If they stop or delay us here in Beijing," Ling said, "then it only gives their comrades that much more time to wring a confession from Mister Thoresen."

"Which is just what we can't afford to let happen," Frost rasped. "Let's go!"

In five minutes the fighting was over—a total of twenty-three of the enemy slain, compared to fourteen dead on the side of the police; more than half of the police casualties were a result of the pair of explosions which the Night Ghosts had triggered at the start of the battle.

Retracing his steps back upstairs to the crime lab to check on Elizabeth Chu'an, Frost was pleased to discover that the female agent had succeeded in removing the jagged piece of glass from the wounded lab assistant's thigh, as well as managing to bring the bleeding to a halt.

"The woman will live," Elizabeth told Frost. "She will bear a scar from the wound, but the memory of how it got there will fade with time."

"That only works sometimes," Frost admitted, thinking to himself of the fine line separating physical scars from emotional ones. "And even when it does fade, the memory's never totally gone altogether. Not from my understanding, at least."

Elizabeth Chu'an regarded him in silence then softly spoke. "From your understanding, Hank Frost, or from your experience?"

"Lady, from where I'm looking at the world, there's no difference."

Chapter Eleven

Having showered and changed into a fresh set of clothes—basic black from his eyepatch down to his G.I. combat boots—Frost wearily reflected that he hadn't looked or felt so good since leaving the States. When he had shaved, there appeared to be more gray decorating his face than the last time he'd noticed, but with the pleasure that came from half-way feeling alive again, not even the added gray in his beard could dampen his spirits.

Taking another ride in the Mayo-Gwantsi, though, was a whole different matter. It put a damper on the physical and mental high he was experiencing. He could tell himself again and again, the No Sweat special had taken them from Canton to Peking with no loss to life or limb, but that didn't matter—the primary reason was that the last few times he had taken to the air it had led to trouble . . .*

Now, as the twin-engine Martin 4-0-4 taxied down the runway and pulled into the dark starlit night, he couldn't help but wonder what manner of stew fate had cooked and waiting for him at the end of the flight. Life and death represented two sides of the same coin. Up until this point in time he had always somehow tossed a

*See, THEY CALL ME THE MERCENARY #15, *The Afghanistan Penetration.*

winning combination—continuing to live his life, while so many others who had challenged him had perished. So far luck had been with him, he sighed, reaching for his cigarettes in anticipation of the all-clear signal from Ling, but as any gambler would admit, he realized, sooner or later the well luck is drawn from runs dry.

Frost sat in his seat, staring out the window, watching the lights of Peking slowly disappear below and behind them, hoping to himself that the Number One gambler in his life kept on winning a whole lot longer ...

"Am I disturbing you, Captain Frost?"

"What?" the one-eyed man came out of his private thoughts with a start.

"Am I disturbing you?"

"No, Ling, you're not. What's up?"

"I have a surprise for you."

"Is that your polite way of telling me we're going to crash?"

But instead of answering, Ling motioned for Frost to follow him to the cargo area at the back of the plane.

"Hey, Ling, we already played this game once. Remember?"

"Yes and no," Ling said, then pulled back a canvas tarp which was covering a wooden crate, this one considerably smaller than the one Frost had seen there earlier. "I trust you are pleased."

Ling stepped aside then as Frost, anxious to discover whether or not he was going to be pleased, broke open the top of the crate, weeding through the packing material that was stuffed inside. He took one look at the contents of the crate and felt a warm smile spread across his face.

"Yeah, Ling, I'm pleased. Thanks."

"I will leave you two to get reacquainted," the S.A.D. agent said and did.

By any standard of measurement the Barnett Commando was the King of the Crossbows. With a 175-pound draw weight prod, cast aluminum stock, solid brass barrel and cocking slides, and fitted with a 4x32mm scope—the Commando was a dream come true. Weighing as much as many assault rifles, the eight-pound Commando was easy to use. Ten-inch groupings at fifty yards for first timers were not out of the ordinary, and for a man of Frost's background, driving one bolt in directly beside another from a comparable distance was not an unreasonable feat.

Frost hefted the Commando into his hands, noting as he did the abundant supply of thin-walled aluminum bolts in the crate below the crossbow. While it was true that fiberglass bolts were also manufactured for the Commando, Frost preferred the aluminum bolts overall because of their greater accuracy and better suitability in "larger" applications. Maybe that was one reason, he imagined, that the Commando was gaining popularity with many of the American SWAT teams.

He returned the Commando to the crate, covered the box with the tarp, and went back to his seat—only to find that O'Hara had taken it.

"How come you're in my seat, Mike?"

"I don't see your name on it, sport."

"Come on. There's at least two dozen empties to choose from."

"I like this one."

Frost sighed and settled into the seat next to O'Hara. "You wanna talk about it?"

"Hmmm?"

"How come you took my seat—and don't tell me it's because you wanted to sit by the window."

"That's not good enough, huh?"

Frost shook his head.

"Ah, okay, you can have your seat back." O'Hara started to get up but Frost stopped him.

"Not until you tell me."

"It's kinda silly."

"Try me."

"It's about Ling. I saw him take you back to the rear of the plane a few minutes ago."

"Yeah, that was me, all right. Why should that upset you?"

O'Hara made a face like he was tasting something sour. "Well, Ling obviously took you back there to give you something—like he did with us earlier today."

"Yeah. So?"

"So, why didn't he have something to give to me, too? After all, we're supposed to be in this thing fifty-fifty, right?"

"Right down the middle, Mike."

"Okay, fine—then where's my present?"

"There isn't one."

"I knew it."

"There isn't one," Frost was quick to point out, "because the one Ling gave to me is supposed to be for the both of us."

"Yeah?" O'Hara's eyes narrowed to suspicious slits. "What is it?"

"A Barnett Commando crossbow—just about the best there is."

O'Hara wrinkled his nose. "A crossbow? What do I need with a crossbow?"

"Ling thought it might come in handy."

"Not for me it won't." The lanky agent from the Federal Bureau of Investigation lifted the left side of his coat and leaned forward, revealing Frost his Cattle Baron Leather Shoulder rig. "All the firepower I need is right here in my Model 29."

"Good. You're not upset, then."

"Nah. You play bows and arrows if you wanna." O'Hara patted his coat into place. "I'll stick with Old Faithful."

"Great. How's about giving me my seat back, then?"

"Too bad, Frost. What can I tell ya? I kinda like riding over the wing."

Frost snapped back, "I'd kinda like you riding under it ..."

Chapter Twelve

The low rumble of wheels touching down on the uneven surface of the dirt airstrip woke Frost from his fitful night's sleep. Back stiff from the awkward position he'd been dozing in, Frost sat upright and rolled his shoulders from side to side, stretching. Looking past O'Hara out the window he could see the growing light of the early morning sunshine splashing across a picture of lush green hills and, beyond those, the rocky silhouette of mountains outlined against the crisp blue sky.

The Mayo-Gwantsi bumped to the end of the airstrip, turned hard to the right, then doubled back in the opposite direction; the action giving Frost a visual image of more hills and mountains, but these much further away in the distance. Separating the view in between was a vast expanse of water cutting over the land like a liquid knife—the Yangtze River, he decided.

Sharing the distinction with the equally famous Yellow River of being one of China's twin lifestreams, the Yangtze was the nation's longest river, beginning at an altitude of some 16,000 feet in the mountains of Quinghai province in the southwest, and draining more than 700,000 square miles of country through it and its tributaries, before finally emptying near Shanghai into the East China Sea.

"Wow," Frost said commented dryly after Ling had briefed him on the Yangtze's statistics. But now, as the

Martin 4-0-4 revved its engines and slowly came to a halt on the airfield, Frost could see that the river was all that Ling had said it was.

"All ashore who's goin' ashore," O'Hara grinned, unbuckling his seat belt and standing. "It looks like my kind of day."

"What kind of day is that?" Frost asked, curious.

"The kind where I'm still alive and kicking."

Frost flipped open his seat belt and stood up. "Can't argue with that ..."

It took less than an hour to unload the plane, after which they settled down to a breakfast before setting off.

"That was swell," O'Hara remarked, finishing the breakfast consisting of a sesame bun, a pair of deep-fried doughsticks, and a bowl of steaming congee—raw grass carp, sliced thin, mixed with soy sauce, cooked peanut oil, shredded ginger and shredded spring onion, then poured boiling hot onto more pieces of fish, and served with shredded lettuce and chopped parsley. "Normally, I'd say to give my compliments to the chef, but since it's past sunrise, that's impossible. He's already been shot."

"You did not like the meal?" Ling asked, somewhat astonished.

"Let me put it to you this way," O'Hara replied with a frown. "No!"

With their gear and weapons safely contained inside several large waterproof duffel bags, then loaded and secured by nylon ties within their four passenger Avon inflatable boat, Frost and the others began their journey on the Yangtze. By Ling's estimation, the trip down the river would take them the balance of the day and on into the following morning, with an overnight stop at a suitable campsite along the way.

While it would have been infinitely easier to have

transferred from the Mayo-Gwantsi to helicopters and simply been flown in to their destination, such a move could have cinched a hasty death for Thoresen. Equipped with a special Bauer radio transmitter, the plan called for Frost and the others to penetrate the enemy's stronghold and radio for an assist only after Thoresen had been rescued or confirmed dead. Triggering the transmitter would launch a unit of helicopters waiting on standby alert to fly with their specially trained Chinese military personnel aboard, and ready to rappel into battle if necessary.

"It's quite basic," Frost summed it up to Ling after the plans were discussed. "If we get in too deep, we radio for help and the choppers pop in and bail us out."

Ling nodded. "That is the essence of the plan."

"And where are all these helicopters supposed to be waitin'?" O'Hara wanted to know.

Elizabeth Chu'an answered. "Close enough to reach us within a reasonable length of time once the signal is sounded, but yet far enough away to escape detection."

"Or in other words—you don't know," Frost concluded.

"That would not be an unfair estimation," Ling agreed.

"Which translates," O'Hara grunted, "that even if the choppers do pick up our signal, it might take them too long to get to us to do us any good. And all that really means is that, for all intents and purposes . . ."

"We're on our own," Frost said.

The one-eyed man left O'Hara to grumble something under his breath that Frost couldn't catch . . .

It was going on two in the afternoon. The sun was hot, there weren't any clouds in the sky, and the weather was tediously warm—the temperature hovering near the high 80s most of the day, Frost guessed. There was a sticky quality to the air that made Frost's clothes feel clammy and slick against his skin and, if it hadn't been for his polarized sunglasses, he would have had a headache.

He and O'Hara had been manning the oars for the last forty-five minutes, their work regulated to doing little more than keeping the Avon flowing with the current. They had veered from their course on the Yangtze to travel on one of the river's many offshoots, this one pulling away from the river and then rejoining it more than twenty miles downstream.

"The map lists the way we are going as a short cut." Ling had shown Frost the squiggly tiny line of blue as it left the Yangtze only to link back up with it again about a quarter-inch down on the map. "By taking this short cut we will save important hours in our journey."

At the time, it had seemed like a good idea to Frost. But now, with the broad expanse of the Yangtze River more than seven miles to their rear, the one-eyed man was having his doubts.

"You notice anything different, O'Hara?"

"Like what, Frost?"

"Like how we seem to be moving faster now than we were a few minutes ago."

"So, what's wrong with that? Going faster is what short cuts are all about."

"I know that, but look." He lifted his oar out of the water, instructing O'Hara to do the same? "See? Even with the oars out of the water we're still picking up speed. I think we'd better," his words froze in his throat and the one-eyed man felt his right eye go wide at what he was seeing. "Holy shit!"

"Oh, brother." O'Hara slapped his oar into the water in a desperate attempt to beach their craft along the shore. Frost, too, thrust his oar into the current, but to no avail. The durable olive-drab Avon inflatable crashed into a wave, spraying water all over them.

A second wave slammed against the boat, threatening to swamp them, as Frost shouted back to Ling, "Some short cut!" Then the Avon inflatable dipped dangerously low, doubling their water speed. To the left and right the rocky shoreline narrowed, dwindling, forming a natural funnel. Suddenly the shoreline and bright sunshine above were gone, giving way to a somber, closed-in canyon, veiled in shadows and roaring with the sound of pounding rapids—powerful waves breaking over the Avon, completely drenching Frost and his crew.

Knowing there was no way to realistically fight the smashing flow of water rushing beneath them, the one-eyed man just tried to keep the Avon from bashing apart against his side of the canyon; O'Hara doing his best to cover the side opposite. A reckless glimpse over his shoulder showed Frost that Elizabeth and Ling had taken up the spare oars in back to defend the rear of the boat as best they could.

The rubberized side of the inflatable fell hard to port, taking on another monster wave, riding the whitewater in a sweeping drive to the left, surging toward the canyon wall to a collision the plastic oars were powerless to prevent. But Frost tried anyway, had to try, bracing the oar against his body, holding it tightly in both hands, striking the wall, the oar bending and snapping in two, Frost losing his balance, leaving his seat, thrown against the canyon wall and back into the boat again as the Avon tilted deep to starboard, shooting for the wall on the opposite side.

"Hank!"

Over the din of the crashing, crushing rapids, Frost heard Elizabeth's anguished cry. He turned, the boat lurching beneath him like something alive, his right hand gripping the seat for support, fingers slipping, another wave washing over the Avon, Frost watching as Elizabeth clawed at the slippery rubberized surface of the boat, the woman falling, spilling helplessly over the side.

Frost leaped, diving for the woman, left hand clutching at a tie line secured to the boat, his right hand outstretched, reaching as far as he could, his fingers closing on her arm as Elizabeth hit the water, dragging the one-eyed man in after her. Water then, tons of it, drowning him, pulling him under, the agonizing strain on his left arm as the tie line snapped taut, making him want to scream, his right hand digging into Elizabeth's flesh, refusing to let go. Frost gasped, his head clearing the surface of the water, lungs sucking for air, water pounding him under again, forcing him down, his mind vaguely aware of the tie line cutting into his skin. Rocks brushed against his feet, dragging him deeper into the water. He kicked away, pulling Elizabeth with him, both of them breaking through the whitewater surface of the rapids, stealing lungfuls of air.

''Frost!''

It was O'Hara—screaming at him from another world—his friend's words were lost as he sank below the surface. For the last time? He didn't know. He was growing weaker, though, losing his strength. Blinded in his good eye now. Everything was dark. His only sensation that of sinking—Elizabeth clamped in the unrelenting vise of his right arm—deeper and deeper.

He had been underwater for centuries. His lungs were to the bursting point. And in the last corner of his consciousness he was faintly aware of a new demand being made of his left arm as something began pulling his body upward, reeling him and Elizabeth in like a couple of fish. He laughed at the idea because, all at once, he had broken through the surface of the water again and he could laugh.

Hands were there, strong hands, reaching for Elizabeth, voices too, calling for him to let go of her, his right arm somehow responding to the command, muscles relaxing, then Elizabeth was gone.

Now his turn. Hands—they had to be O'Hara's—gripping his shoulders, grabbing and pulling, lifting his body weight out of the water, over the side of the Avon inflatable, back into the boat.

All he could do was concentrate on his breathing. It felt so good to breathe. He coughed, spitting up water, gallons of it, he thought. His heart was beating like a kettle-drum working overtime. And slowly he began to come back to earth, to calm down.

"How ... how is ..." he coughed again, filling the Avon's interior with, what seemed to Frost, an ocean full of water. "How is Elizabeth? Is she all right?"

His right eye opened, not blind after all, seeing Ling and O'Hara, his buddy from the FBI telling him, "She's just as soaked as you are, sport. But she'll live. And so will you."

Red and black floaters played across his eye as he started blacking out. "Thanks for the warning ..." He wanted to say something else ...

"Tell me, Agent O'Hara," Ling began. It was ten after eight, according to the Rolex on Frost's left wrist, and they had been at the campsite only long enough to start a fire for Ling to boil water for tea. "What is the date of your birth?"

"It's not a classified secret," O'Hara responded, then answered Ling's question. "How come you want to know?"

But instead of replying directly to O'Hara's question,

the S.A.D. agent looked across the fire to O'Hara and said, "It is just as I thought. You are a Pig."

"Now, hold on there a minute, Ling. You and I might not agree with each other's political beliefs, but that's still no reason for going rude on me."

Ling smiled. "You misunderstood, Mike," he said, Frost noting that he was using O'Hara's given name again. "When I call you a 'Pig' I am not doing so in the derogatory sense ..."

"But according to Chinese astrological signs," Elizabeth Chu'an told him.

"That is correct," Ling said. "Governed by the date of your birth—you were born in the Year of the Pig. I, myself, am a Horse."

"I'm as hungry as one," O'Hara shot back. "So long as we aren't having cobra or raw fish for supper." He looked at Elizabeth. "What sign were you born under?"

She grinned, "The Year of the Snake."

"That figures," O'Hara commented.

"Are you sure you've got Mike's year right, Ling?" Frost asked.

"I am positive. Why?"

The one-eyed man laughed. "I know O'Hara better than you do—seems more like a Rat to me." O'Hara didn't laugh ...

"Thank you for saving my life."

"I didn't have much of a choice."

"How is that?"

"Easy. When you started falling overboard, you called my name. I guess I felt obligated."

"I'm grateful that you did," she confessed. "Still, it is interesting that you would risk your own life to save that of an enemy spy."

"You're not the 'enemy' now, Elizabeth. And the only job you're doing is the same one I am. This go round—

we're partners. When and if it ever works out that we come up against each other and you're on this side of the fence, and I'm on that side . . . well, I'll decide what I'm gonna do about it when the time comes.''

They had left O'Hara and Ling sitting in front of the fire, along with most of their water-logged gear. O'Hara and Ling had been arguing the political merits of social reform when Frost, needing to make his muscles work, and Elizabeth, wrapped in a blanket, opted for a walk in lieu of listening to politics.

Frost had regained consciousness in the Avon inflatable about ten minutes after blacking out. The first thing he had noticed was that his eyepatch had miraculously stayed in place throughout his ordeal in the water. The second thing he realized upon opening his eye was that his head was cradled in Elizabeth's lap. Her hair was stringly and plastered to her scalp, her skin was wrinkled from exposure to the water, and her eyes were puffed and swollen—yet at that exact moment, knowing they had both beaten the odds of survival—the sight of waking to Elizabeth Chu'an holding him was— simply beautiful.

Now, as Frost sat on a fallen log, talking with her, he couldn't help thinking to himself how incredibly lovely Elizabeth Chu'an really was.

''Do you mind if I ask you a question, Hank?''

''As long as it doesn't involve handstands or backflips—shoot.'' His back ached.

''I hesitated asking earlier because I did not know you well enough. It would have been impolite. But now that we have shared our brush with death, such formality seems out of place.''

''Go on,'' he encouraged, moving his left arm in a circular motion, trying to work some of the stiffness from his shoulder. ''What is it you want to know?''

97

"It is—about your eye."

"How I lost it, you mean?"

She nodded. "If you don't mind."

"Not if you want to hear it. It all began the first time I visited Los Angeles. Not much of a story really. It was in the summer and the smog that day was murder. I wasn't out of the airport for more than a minute before the severity of the dirty air hit me hard, some kind of allergic reaction to the pollution. Anyway, I started sneezing. And not just little sneezes, mind you, but real glass-breakers. From a distance I must have sounded like a car backfiring.

"I got a cab and told him I wanted to go to Hollywood, to a theatre there called the Pantages—which was where I was supposed to meet a friend. Well, I hopped in the cab and we took off, getting close to five miles out of the airport when—I couldn't help it—I sneezed. All at once the cab driver slammed on the brakes and jumped out of the car. Wouldn't you know it? He thought my sneeze was a flat tire on his cab.

"Finally, I got to Hollywood, paid the cab fare, and then waited for my friend to show. Two hours later I was still waiting and my friend was nowhere to be seen. Naturally, I got angry, but because it was getting late, I was also getting hungry. Figuring I'd grab myself a bite to eat and then come back and wait some more, I started looking for a restaurant. As luck would have it, right around the corner was a place called Zorba's Chinese— which is typical of how restaurants are named in California.

"Just as I opened the door to go in I felt a tickling sensation on the tip of my nose, like another big sneeze was about to break loose. Before that could happen though, I braced my finger under my nose, held my breath, and counted to three. Like magic, I got rid of the sneeze.

"I went into the restaurant, sat down and ordered my meal—pressed almond chicken over rice. Zorba must've had it cooking on one of the back burners, because in a couple of seconds, dinner was served. Normally, when partaking of oriental dishes I usually use a knife and fork, but for some reason that day I was feeling brave. That's why I told my waiter to take away the silverware and bring me a pair of chopsticks.

"The waiter happened to have a spare pair in his back pocket, so I took them off his hands and started to eat. At least that's what I tried doing. But no matter how I worked 'em, I couldn't pick any food up with those chopsticks to save my life. Trial and error and a cold dinner later I got the hang of it. Before you could say Zorba Robinson I was gripping the chopsticks like an expert and there, held between them, was a succulent piece of pressed almond chicken. I raised the chopsticks from my plate, started bringing the piece of chicken to my mouth, and then ..."

"You sneezed?" Elizabeth guessed.

"Who's telling this story?"

"You didn't sneeze?"

"Of course I did. The doctor said later the reason the sneeze was so big was because of the one I had prevented earlier outside the restaurant. Whatever the reason—when I went 'Ahhh', I threw my head way back, and then when the 'chooooo' part of the sneeze hit me. I threw my head forward and—well ..."

The woman laughed, a grown-up little girl laugh. "That is a very sad tale, Hank."

"Every word is true—no kiddin'." He rotated his left shoulder again.

"You are in pain?"

"Pulled a muscle, I think, back when O'Hara was reeling us in out of the water. My arm was supporting

99

both of our weights and then some."

"Then I will make it feel better."

And before Frost could protest, Elizabeth, clutching her blanket loosely about her, moved behind the one-eyed man, her fingers reaching out in a soothing caress to massage the hurt from his body.

"Ahhh," Frost sighed.

"Don't tell me you are going to sneeze?"

"No," Frost had to smile, "it's not that. What you heard was an 'ahhh' of relief. What you are doing feels great." He closed his eye and relaxed, enjoying the release of tension her fingertips provided, feeling her lean into him, pressing the front of her body against his back.

"Elizabeth . . ."

"Shhh," she silenced him. "It would be a simple matter, Hank Frost, for me to allow the blanket I am wearing to fall to the ground. I could spread it over the earth, and then you could have me. We could make love."

Frost stood, turning to face her, his hands reaching out, pulling her into his arms, holding her close against his chest, her chin tilting upward, a smile on her lips. He was kissing her, tasting the sweetness of her mouth, his tongue dueling with hers, heat between them.

"Elizabeth," Frost softly whispered her name, breaking their kiss, drawing her even closer into his arms.

Frost kissed her again, his hands exploring her under the blanket.

"Frost—the damned grenades—all wet!"

It was O'Hara—as Frost stepped away from the girl, starting back toward the fire, he said it to himself—"Shit!"

Chapter Thirteen

Back on the Yangtze early the next morning Frost was relieved to discover that Ling had no additional "short-cuts" planned for the rest of their run down the river.

"It is lamentable but true, Captain, that the map I referred to yesterday made no mention of turbulent waters."

"We didn't just imagine them, Ling." Frost stretched, letting his bare feet push against the side of the Avon inflatable—his feet were bare because his combat boots had yet to dry out to his satisfaction. "Maybe that map we're using is no good. It's certainly inaccurate."

"That fact has not escaped me," Ling admitted, "and so, once we have finished with our business concerning your Mr. Thoresen, I shall bring the matter of the map's inconsistencies to the attention of those who will best benefit from such knowledge."

"Speaking of knowledge," O'Hara cut in, directing his comment to Ling, "I've been wondering about our mode of transportation here." Frost was impressed—"mode" was a new word for O'Hara. O'Hara slapped the side of the boat. "This olive-drab version of the Avon is strictly U.S. Government issue. How did you happen to get it?"

"That's an easy one, Mike—he got it from a friend of a friend of a friend. Right, Ling?"

"One and the same, Captain Frost. One and the same . . ."

By mid-morning they had reached the area of the river where they were to beach the Avon and continue inland on foot. They floated in as near to the shore as possible and then Frost—because he was barefoot already—jumped into the water and helped pull the rubberized boat the rest of the way in. Although noon wouldn't arrive for another two hours, the temperature was showing every indication of being hotter than the day before. The sun was gathering strength in a blue cloudless sky, and the air was thick with the combined scents of the vast Yangtze and the lush mountain forest which grew almost to the water's edge.

Frost and the others pulled the Avon ashore, then set about unloading the weapons and equipment, including two sets of scuba diving gear, a pair of handheld spearguns, and finally a small rectangular-shaped case that Ling removed last, carrying it over to where O'Hara was busy securing the Metalifed and Mag-Na-Ported Model 29 into his shoulder holster.

"Whatcha got there, Ling?" O'Hara asked.

"In the short time we have worked together," Ling explained, "I have come to realize that—political and cultural differences notwithstanding—you and I are very much alike."

"Yeah, how come?"

"Let the man talk," Frost told his pal.

"Thank you." Ling smiled, then proceeded. "We are alike primarily because we both appreciate the importance of loyalty, whether it be to the nation of our birth, to our friends, or even to the very weapons we depend upon to save our lives when the need arises. We are loyal to them all for, once having made a commitment, our respect to that commitment never wavers.

We are traditionalists, you and I, a vanishing breed in the modern world." The S.A.D. agent lifted the rectangular-shaped case into O'Hara's hands. "We resist change in our lives for we know that, for every portion of change that we accept, an equal portion of our own true self is lost to us forever."

"What's in the box, Ling?"

"It is a gift from me to you, Mike O'Hara, but knowing you as I know myself, I will not be offended if you choose not to accept it."

"Why not let me see what it is first," O'Hara told him. "Then let me decide if I want to keep it or not."

Frost was as curious as O'Hara. Standing beside Elizabeth, he watched while Ling watched the tall man from the FBI calmly set the case on the ground the open it.

"Don't tell me," O'Hara's voice was quiet, but obviously bubbling rich with excitement below the surface. "You got this from that same friend of a friend of a friend of yours. Right?"

"Perhaps," was all Ling chose to reveal.

"Is he pleased?" Elizabeth whispered to Frost.

"And how," the one-eyed man murmured, then said to O'Hara. "Well, Mike, are you gonna be the one to take it out of the case, or is that going to be my job?"

"No way, Frost. This baby's mine." And with that O'Hara, pride shining like a high-beam headlight across his face, gently removed the weapon from its case and held it out for all to see.

It was a Heckler & Koch G-11 caseless gun—a prototype of which O'Hara had told Frost he'd seen demonstrated and had the opportunity to use at an ADPA* Symposium on Small Arms held at Ft. Benning, Georgia.

*American Defense Preparedness Association

Weighing in at just under ten pounds, the H&K G-11 was an assault rifle whose outward appearance Flash Gordon would have liked. Constructed for the most part of high-grade gray plastic, the G-11 featured a totally in-line stock, completely devoid of protrusions. Its scope tube—utilizing a 1x optical sight—and scope mount itself were nicely integrated as part of the receiver molding to also serve as the gun's carrying handle.

The G-11's magazine—holding 50 in-line caseless 4.7x21mm cartridges—was mounted on a horizontal bar atop the barrel, extending backward from the muzzle to the receiver, and was inserted or detached up forward. Offering the option of single, three-round, or full auto bursts, the futuristic-looking H-K delivered its ammo at a cyclic rate near or better than 1,000 rpm, with a muzzle velocity of 3,100 fps.

"Not too shabby," Frost joked.

"Not by a mile," O'Hara was fast to agree, then said to Ling. "It's a super gift. I don't know what else to say." O'Hara tucked the G-11, barrel down, under his left arm, then crossed to shake Ling's hand. "Thanks."

"You are most welcome," Ling returned, accepting O'Hara's hand, shaking it firmly, then saying to no one in particular. "Shall we be on our way, then?"

"Why not?" Frost answered, slipping on his socks and then testing the insoles of his combat boots to make sure they were dry enough to wear. They were. "If I had to pick a day to go hiking through the mountains hauling half my body weight in gear—this is the kind of day I'd pick."

The trail began inland as soon as they entered the forest, less than one hundred yards from the Yangtze's shoreline. Going from left to right the dirt trail, more of a path at times, led them on a zigzag pattern that steadily moved upward, taking them higher into the mountains and deeper into potentially hostile territory.

Even with Ling setting the pace of their climb, the going was slow—out of necessity and the concern for safety. Transporting their equipment in backpacks, as well as a two man litter-system that Ling and O'Hara were carrying, they often discovered that the trail they were following had diminished to little more than a narrow ledge.

"The kind of trail where, if you fall off it," Frost grimly noted, "you only bounce once, and that's when you hit the ground."

Rest breaks were taken every thirty minutes for five minutes each before pushing on again. At half past one they stopped for a late lunch in a cool pocket of shade provided by a cragging outcropping of rock. Ling dipped into his shoulder bag and produced a pint-sized styrofoam container for each of them—a meal of cold rice, a sprinkling of vegetables, plus several pieces of barbecued meat that O'Hara complained tasted like it "might have come from any dozen different breeds of dogs and cats!"

They washed down their meal with water from their canteens, then Ling had everyone back on the trail, moving nearer to their destination.

By Frost's estimation they had covered close to five miles, making their best progress since their last rest break, when the trail began heading down. After that the going was so much easier that they elected to skip the next rest period in favor of getting out of the mountains that much faster. Eventually, the mountains became hills and before long, the hills gave way to a dense forest packed with more trees per square foot than Frost had ever seen.

The trail seemed to evaporate once it hit the forest, but an eagle-eyed Ling—Frost knew he would—soon picked it up again and had them on their way. Two winding miles and more than an hour later Ling quietly called the procession to a halt.

First secreting their belongings well off the trail behind a high barrier of bushes and trees, Ling cautioned them to silence and then led them further up the trail, traveling less than a quarter mile before the trail left the forest and disappeared altogether—vanishing onto the rock and sand beach of an immense lake.

From where he stood with the others, shielded from observation by the protection of the trees, Frost gauged the body of water before him to be at least one-and-a-half miles wide. Rising from the middle of the lake was an island of vast proportions, and on the island—an enormous fortress-like enclosure—the enemy stronghold they had come to attack.

If the Lung-men temple had resembled something off a set of a film, the impressive structure Frost was contemplating now was vintage Cecil B. DeMille. With walls of stone and wood more than fifty feet high, the four corners of the fortress were great polygonal towers rising another twenty feet into the air. Armed guards could be seen manning these towers, with additional guards posted at various intervals along the walls.

Frost knew there had to be more buildings inside, but the only one visible from his position was a three-story affair in the center of the compound whose broad flat roof provided an ideal landing site for helicopters.

"A piece of cake," Frost said. "It'll be a snap, no problem at all—if we had a hundred commandos backing us up. On our own, though, getting in there to get Thoresen out is going to be a bitch." He turned to Ling. "Does that crazy map of yours have a name for this lake?"

"Yes," Ling nodded, not bothering to consult his map. "In English, you would call it Heaven's Lake."

"Wonderful," Frost nodded. "You hear that, Elizabeth? Tonight we gotta cross Heaven, so we can get to hell ..."

Chapter Fourteen

It was a full moon, hanging in the black velvet of the evening sky like a polished silver coin. It was bright outside, too much so—Frost decided—for while the full moon would make it easier for them to see to work their way into the enemy fortress, it would also drastically increase the risk of being spotted by guards manning the walls. "'Dark of the moon' my rear end," he groaned.

Having gotten his compass orientations earlier in the day, Frost had spent the balance of the afternoon inspecting his weapons, cleaning them, basically doing everything within his power to insure that he could depend upon his arsenal one hundred percent, and everything in his power to keep from thinking about the mission.

Now, wearing a wet suit, and with most of his weapons safely tucked inside watertight bags, it was almost time to leave.

"Ya got everythin', Frost?" O'Hara had been acting jumpy ever since the sun went down. "Make sure because once you get over there it's not like you can turn around and head back at the drop of a hat."

"You're worse than a little old lady, O'Hara, but yeah—I got everything, thanks." The one-eyed man bent and inserted a ten-inch tanto knife into the sheath attached to the right leg of his wet suit pants. Along with the knife, the only other weapon he would have access to in the water would be a hand-held speargun, cocked and ready to fire, with three spare bolts for the gun strapped with velcro to the left forearm of his wet suit jacket. "I'm all dressed up with someplace to go. Give me a hand."

With O'Hara holding it up like Frost was putting on a coat, the one-eyed man eased his arms into the straps of the backplate to which the air tank was secured. Frost hefted the weight into place, shifted the harness on each side until it felt comfortable, then tightened the straps to his liking. "I usually take a 42 regular," he said, "but this will have to do. How do I look?"

O'Hara laughed. "Like you hopped out of a comic book. Whatta ya expect?"

Frost adjusted the pressure gauge/depth gauge hose so it rode near the left side of his waist, a few inches up from the lead-weighted belt he was wearing. "You wanna tell me why you've been so antsy ever since it got dark."

"Not really, no."

"Okay, don't tell me. But when I'm in the middle of the lake, running around on that island, probably fighting everybody and their Chinese cousin to stay alive, and I can't quite concentrate on what I'm doing because you had to be selfish and not tell me what's bugging you—well, it won't be on my hands if something goes wrong."

"That's bullshit and you know it, Frost, but if you really want to know the truth, I've been pacing back and forth the last few hours, like some animal trapped in a cage 'cause, aww, hell . . . 'cause you're gettin' ready to leave and I'm not goin' with ya."

"Aww, come on, O'Hara, you know the plan. Elizabeth and I are going in together because that's what we're trained to do."

"But I ..." O'Hara pushed his lantern jaw out, starting to protest.

"I didn't say you weren't capable of going in too. Of course, you are. But the way we've got it set to ride is right on target. You said it yourself—Elizabeth is one of the best in the business."

"Yeah, but ..."

"Uh uh, yeah but nothin', Mike. If we can't rescue Thoresen without an assist we'll trigger the transmitter to alert the choppers. When you hear them coming in, Ling is suppose to set off a flare to signal them of your location. One of the 'copters will pick you both up, and you'll get to make the trip to the island First Class. If ya ask me, I'm the one that should be griping."

"Why's that?"

Frost held up his face mask. "What you're looking at here is an open and shut clear-cut case of discrimination. And if we manage to squeak through this mess in one piece, I'm gonna raise all kinds of flack when I get back to the States."

"Yeah, how come?"

"Easy. Everybody knows you don't give a one-eyed skin diver a diving mask like this—you give him a diving monocle."

"Well—you just confirmed it for me, Frost. You're nuts—the Mayor of Cashew City and then some."

"Of course I am," Frost grinned. "Now hand me my flippers ..."

Chapter Fifteen

The water closed over his face, blotting out the silvery coin of the moon, making him immediately more aware of each breath that he took. He leaned forward, felt himself start to fall, and began to kick—working his fins in an up and down motion, propelling him further away from the shore, dragging the waterproof bags containing his weapons in tow.

Next to Frost, gliding gracefully beside him, was Elizabeth Chu'an, wearing a jet black wet suit and armed with the same kind of knife and speargun Frost was using. There was no question in his mind that Elizabeth was one of the bravest women he'd met. They were on their way to meet possible death, and yet, as they were making their final preparations to leave, Elizabeth might have been getting ready to go shopping for all of the outward emotion she exhibited.

"I can understand why you might want to keep a tight grip on your nerves," Frost had said to her. "But it's almost like you've shut down that part of your consciousness until all of this is over."

"In a way you are right," she confided. "I am a firm believer of regulating my fears so that they will not conflict with my duty."

"Well, you're doing one helluva job of it. I wouldn't guess you had a frightened bone in your body in a million years."

"And yet I am frightened, Hank—terrified. Before I embark on any high risk mission the fear of what I will be letting myself in for overwhelms me, devouring me like a hungry beast starving for food."

"So," Frost had wondered, "why, after all this time, hasn't it beaten you?"

"Oh, it has—many times. But the strength fear knows is temporal, living only as long as your doubts and worries allow. Fear had always been the victor with me—in the beginning, but then I set my doubts and worries and questions without answers aside, and I conquer fear." She had looked at him, then, more beautiful than a memory would ever serve to recall, and she had asked, "Surely, Hank, with the path through life you have chosen to take, surely you must have known fear."

"All the time."

"And conquered it, too?"

"Well," he'd confessed, "I'm still working on that part . . ."

Frost had expected the lake to be impenetrably dark once they reached their predetermined diving level of thirty feet, so he was surprised to learn that—at that depth—the brightness of the moon above still offered them some degree of illumination to guide their way. And it was because of this extra light, afforded them by the moon's reflected glow, that they were able to draw back from their course before colliding headlong into the net.

It had been ages since he had seen one like it, but Frost readily recognized the net as the kind originally used years ago to snare submarines. Made of a durable wire mesh, a closer examination of the net revealed a slender cord weaving in and out of its links, all the way up to the surface of the water. That told Frost that the net was rigged to set off an alarm should someone the size of a human bump into it.

He looked down, hoping to see the bottom of the net, but as far as he could tell its wire-mesh fabric dropped all the way to the lake's floor. He considered momentarily the possibility of swimming to the bottom and trying to dig under the net, but just as quickly gave up the idea. Even if they managed to dig out a space large enough for them to pass through below the net, the odds were great that electronic sensors had probably been embedded in the lake bottom to activate an alarm as well.

Signaling for Elizabeth to follow, Frost backed off away from the net and began swimming west, to the left, moving parallel to the wire-mesh barrier. Thirty yards west the net came to an end and another one like it began—stretching off into the void, lost and out of sight. It was not this second net that interested Frost, however, but the measurable distance between where it began and net number one ended.

Frost judged the distance separating the two nets was anywhere from two-and-a-half to three feet—plenty of room to squeeze through, if they were careful. He was preparing to give it a try then when, much to the one-eyed man's frustration, the water about them appeared to shift—as though fed by the current of some underground source—and the gap between the two nets closed to less than six inches apart. He was ready to signal to Elizabeth that they should swim back to the right to seek another way through, when the shift in current came again and the gap reopened.

Motioning for Elizabeth to wait, Frost gingerly approached the space between the nets, mentally tossing a coin in his mind to decide whether or not to take the chance. The toss came up in his favor and he made his move—he mentally and physically shrugged, cautiously swimming forward between the nets, ever so gently pulling his bags of weapons behind him.

He made it through.

If he had been standing out in the open air Frost would have laughed out loud. He had breached the first of the enemy's defenses successfully. Now all he had to do was help Elizabeth get through too.

Frost saw her on the opposite side of the nets, treading in place, less than ten feet away—the gap between the pair of nets tempting and teasing them both. Frost nodded, made his decision, then motioned for Elizabeth to join him.

She waved, indicating that she understood, and started swimming for the gap, preparing to slide her body between the nets when, without warning, the invisible current of the lake struck again, bringing the nets together, nearly trapping Elizabeth before she could escape.

Frost swore to himself, cursing the net. They were losing precious time. Each minute of delay was one minute less of the oxygen supply they might need to reach the island. But while he debated what to do next, the decision was made for him as the nets drew apart again, as fast as they had closed a moment before.

Without waiting to be told to, Elizabeth started through, kicking her legs against the water, easing her way between the two nets, making it halfway when Frost felt it, sensed it—the current again!

Moving as swiftly as he could, Frost swam for the woman, reaching for her, his right hand clamping on her left wrist, pulling then, moving away, taking her with him, dragging her through the gap between the nets as it began to disappear, to close around her body.

Then Elizabeth was through and Frost abandoned

her, letting her go and turning to retrieve the water-proof bag she'd been towing, grabbing its line, tugging hard with all of his strength, bringing the bag to his side of the net just as the gap shut behind it.

He was still congratulating himself for their small victory when Elizabeth suddenly clutched him by the arm, bringing him to an abrupt halt. She had seen them before he had, but as Frost let his right eye strain to pierce the moonlit shadows ahead, he saw them—countless small anti-personnel mines, chained to the bottom of the lake, rising to various heights.

With the alarm nets behind them and the mines blocking their way in front, Frost could easily picture the consequences of striking one of the mines as giving him what he had heard referred to once as a 4-B send-off—Bump, Boom, and Bye-Bye.

Wishing desperately he could stop and light up a cigarette, Frost signaled for Elizabeth to follow and began to swim forward.

Chapter Sixteen

The inside of his wet suit felt like a sauna as Frost shook his head, trying to remove the bead of sweat clinging to his eye. But it was no good. All the shaking was doing was giving him a headache, and the drop of sweat was staying in his eye, stinging it, blurring his vision. And that was the last thing in the world he needed.

Surrounded on all sides, including above and below, by scores of the anti-personnel mines, he and Elizabeth had worked their perilous way across half of the underwater mind field unscathed. Which was terrific. What didn't exactly set his heart singing, though, was the realization that instead of the density of the mines thinning out as he had hoped, there were more of them now than ever before.

Frost had seen enough of what mines like these could do during his tour of duty in Viet Nam. A friend of his had been one of four U.S. sailors killed in 1966 when a single VC-planted mine had taken out their Swift Boat in the Gulf of Siam. If a single mine could cause so much havoc then, it made him shudder to think of the total potential for destruction the mine field they were in presented. One false move and that would be it— detonation, possibly even a chain reaction detonation of all the mines planted along the lake bottom, and he would instantly cease to be Hank Frost, the one-eyed man, to become instead head spokesman for Henry Stimson Frost Fish Food, Inc.

He stared ahead at the constantly shifting multi-level obstacle course, decided upon what he considered to be the best route through the maze, and swam forward, keeping his weapon bags tucked under his arm— Elizabeth following behind and doing the same.

At times the distance separating them from the mines could be measured in inches; at others their leeway rose by as much as several feet. The strain on his nerves was unbearable. Having no way to tell for sure how old or how sensitive the conical-shaped mines were, for all Frost knew it would take next to nothing to detonate one of them.

His right eye responded to the sweat stinging its surface by filling with tears, washing the eye, and returning his vision to normal. They had less than twenty-five feet to go. Beyond that the lake bottom appeared clear and free of any further surprises to get in their way.

Seeing that he had approximately five feet to swim before reaching the next mine, Frost swiveled his head around and glanced over his shoulder—checking on Elizabeth.

The one-eyed man froze, a feeling like ice along his spine, racing through his system.

Elizabeth was caught, snagged into going nowhere by the tow line attached to her weapons bag. Somehow, the line had become entangled in one of the chains supporting a mine, and Elizabeth had no choice but to tread softly in place, unable to move away or to let the bag drop.

Using hand signals to caution Elizabeth to remain as still as possible, he traced the path of the tie line from the weapons bag to where its knotted-end had become lodged inside a partially broken link of chain. To try and work the knotted-end free would have been suicide—the effort necessary to do so more than ample to jar the mine to life.

No, he thought, messing with the knot was not the way.

Keeping his own equipment well away from the dangerously swaying chain, Frost reached down to the sheath on his right leg and removed the ten-inch tanto knife. Holding the razor-sharp hollow ground blade by its curved black handle, Frost counted to three for luck, and prepared to saw through the line—his left hand gripping the part of the line closest to the chain.

The tanto severed the tow line in one smooth slice—freeing Elizabeth, and leaving Frost to slowly release the tension on the line's knotted-end. Gradually he fed the line out, letting the chain find its own point of ease. When it looked like the chain didn't want to fight against the line any more, Frost let it go.

He breathed a long sigh and allowed his arms and fins to carry him back, away from the mine Elizabeth had snagged. His eye was full of sweat again, but he didn't really care. What he did care about was getting the hell out of the mine field in one piece, rather than a bunch of tiny ones.

He resheathed the knife, then swam toward Elizabeth, squeezing her hand in his, before taking up the lead again, carefully threading a course through what remained of the treacherous mine field. Twenty feet more. Fifteen. Ten to go. Five. And then it was over—they were through!

Frost worked his fins to put another twenty-five feet of breathing space between him and the underwater mines, then made a quick visual check to make sure Elizabeth was behind him, which she was. He got their bearings straight on the compass he wore on his right wrist, then inspected the time on the luminous dial of his Rolex. Incredibly, less than twelve minutes had elapsed since they had first entered the water, but to the one-eyed man it seemed more like twelve years.

Elizabeth was treading in place to his right, and as Frost looked around to let her know he was ready to continue, he almost swallowed his mouthpiece—five frogmen were swimming in their direction. At first the divers were visible in the filtered moonlight from above only as hazy, indistinct shapes, but as they swam nearer it became disturbingly evident that the scuba equipped guards were armed and combat ready.

It was obvious to Frost as he watched the guards approach—traveling in single file, casually shifting their heads from one side to the other as they advanced—that theirs was most likely a routine patrol, and not part of a larger contingent sent out to scour the lake for them in particular. He knew the guards hadn't spotted them yet, but was also aware that luck like that couldn't last forever.

It didn't.

The diver swimming at the head of the group suddenly pointed in their direction, broke formation, and began charging forward—a full-sized speargun clutched in his arms, the four other divers trying to catch up.

Frost and Elizabeth split, swimming in opposite directions, dividing the lead guard's attention, presenting two moving targets instead of just one.

Frost saw that the lead guard had opted to hunt him down first and save Elizabeth for later, the obvious tactical decision on the guard's behalf since Frost was physically larger than Elizabeth, and so would make an easier target to hit.

The spear from the gun shot wide and to the left, missing Frost, the one-eyed man reversing in the water and launching his own attack. The enemy diver let the empty speargun fall, frantically reaching for a knife, Frost stopping him with a shot from the miniature hand-held speargun—straight through the lens of the guard's face mask.

Frost spun from the body as the remaining four guards separated—two coming for him—the second pair chasing after Elizabeth. The first guard was raising his speargun to fire when Frost grabbed at the shoulders of the guard's already dead comrade, using the body to block the spear as it launched.

There was a thudding sound. The scuba diver's spear struck the dead guard's unresisting flesh, plowing into the stomach, under the ribcage, and out the back through the spine, its dull black point coming to a halt less than an inch from Frost's lead weighted belt.

Frost pushed the twice dead body aside and snatched the tanto knife from his leg sheath just as the man who'd fired the speargun moved in. A long-bladed diving knife was clamped in his right fist.

On land the diver brandishing the knife might have been an expert with the weapon, but Frost doubted it. What was highly more likely was that the knife had been issued to the diver on short notice, and that the man had been given little or no formal training using it. An awkward slash the man made with the blade confirmed Frost's guess.

Circling in the water so that guard number two couldn't get off a shot without running the risk of killing the first man, Frost pulled away from the sluggish slash and then lashed out with the tanto, driving straight in, thrusting below the diver's outstretched hand, plunging up to the hilt into the man's chest. The man thrashed in agony as Frost pulled the blade free, then suddenly became still as death overtook him, a dark cloud of blood in the water.

There was no time to reload the mini-speargun, and with the first man dead, the second man wouldn't have to hold his fire. But the second guard had other ideas, Frost realized. Charging through the water, grasping his speargun like it could have been a rifle behind a bayonet, the lone diver swam forward, legs kicking fast behind him, the point of the spear-tip he wielded aimed at Frost's chest. Twisting sharply to the left to avoid the attack, Frost forced his right wrist to the side of the barbed spear as it passed, successfully deflecting the shaft, but the impact of doing so loosened his grip on the tanto.

The blade slipped from his fingers, totally useless now, the guard swinging away and around to have a fresh go with the speargun. He was completing the maneuver when Frost tore away one of the spare shafts for the mini-speargun, and attacked—stabbing into the guard as he turned, punching the shaft deep into the man's unprotected side.

Reflexively, the wounded man's finger twitched on the trigger of his speargun, launching the spear and sending it shooting through the water on a direct collision course with the mine field. Frost tensed, waiting for the explosion he was helpless to prevent, then relaxed as the spear lost its momentum and slipped in a dive to the bottom of the lake.

The guard Frost had stabbed was trying to remove the source of the pain eating at his side when Frost—grabbing another of the spares for the mini—drove the nine-inch spike into the man's belly. Blood seeped from the wound in his gut, the eyes wide behind the mask, wide in death.

Frost shoved the man away, then quickly reloaded the hand-held speargun with his last spare bolt. Elizabeth was approximately twenty feet away, wrestling in the moonlit depths of the lake with one of her adversaries. The first diver who had gone after her was floating nearby, speared through the neck.

The diver fighting Elizabeth was preparing to work a knife the size of a small machete into the woman's abdomen. Frost, pulling himself through the water, placed the business end of the mini-spear up to the killer's right ear and fired—the shaft rocketed into the ear, through the brain, bursting from the skull on the opposite side; the dead man's hand flexed open and released the knife which he no longer needed.

Frost watched the knife as it drifted out of sight, then signaled to Elizabeth with the raised thumb of his right hand. The inside of his wet suit felt like an oven.

Chapter Seventeen

Tying the bodies together with the straps from the dead guards' air tanks, and then weighting them down with some of the lead from each of their weight belts, Frost and Elizabeth got back on course, moving underwater to the eastern side of Heaven Lake's island. Frost had no way of knowing for sure when the members of the slain scuba patrol would be missed, but guessed it wouldn't be for at least another half hour. Weighting the bodies as they had would prevent them from floating to the surface for some time, and keep the mystery behind their disappearance going that much longer.

As they swam along, the moonlight above shimmering through the water like dozens of ghostly fingers, Hank Frost felt the urge to laugh. In the past twenty minutes, since leaving O'Hara and Ling on the shore, they had bypassed the security nets, swam through the middle of an underwater mine field, and fought to the death with five enemy guards. All that and the bulk of their journey was still to come. There was a joke in there somewhere, but at the moment it escaped him.

Five minutes later they reached a point where Frost estimated the eastern side of the island would be, and they headed west, swimming in that direction two minutes more, the moonlight seeming to brighten with each foot they gained. Then the lake bottom began curving upward, and when it was only ten feet beneath them, Frost gave the signal to surface.

Eager to be out of the water and back on land, but aware that their departure from the lake would be visible from the fortress walls if anyone were watching—Frost bobbed gently to the surface, Elizabeth doing likewise—both softly treading the water with their fins to remain in place.

Frost's sense of direction, he was gratified to learn, had been on the money. His face mask rising above the waterline only high enough for his right eye to see, the island's craggy beach—barely six feet wide—and the tall eastern wall of the enemy stronghold immediately ahead were almost a welcome sight.

With Elizabeth beside him, and without disturbing the surface of the lake with any unnecessary splashing, Frost swam slowly forward, drawing nearer to the island until he could feel his fins touch bottom.

So far so good.

He eased his swim fins off his feet, glanced up to make sure none of the guards posted were visible—none were—then walked from the water to the base of the wall, clinging to the darkness afforded him by the branches of a short tree. Elizabeth repeated his actions to the letter and, seconds later, joined him under the canopy of the tree.

The first thing Frost did when he took off his face mask was to wipe away the stinging sweat from his eye. That task completed, he and Elizabeth took it in turns, each helping the other get out of their gear—loosening straps, slipping out of the backplates holding the air tanks in position, undoing the weight belts, and finally stripping out of their wet suits, under which both were wearing identical black linen uniforms supplied by Ling. The outfits, now free of the restrictions imposed by the wet suits, were loose fitting without being baggy, and permitted comfortable movement in all directions. From a distance, Frost hoped, they would resemble to the casual observer the same attire worn by the Night Ghosts.

The one-eyed man shivered as he set his wet suit jacket and then his wet suit pants down on the ground next to his scuba tank. After boiling in the wet suit for what had seemed like hours, it was a shock to have his skin breathing again.

He worked his fingers on the air tank's valve, cutting it off, then whispered quietly to Elizabeth, "For a while there I didn't think we had a Chinese chance in ... well, I mean, after what we just went through, it's pretty tough to believe we made it."

"I too had my doubts, Hank, especially there in the mine field when I was caught on the chain. I was conquering fear with each passing heartbeat."

"Yeah, well we made it."

She bit at her lower lip. "How long before the guards from the underwater patrol we killed are discovered, do you think?"

Frost gave her his guess, adding, "But their being found doesn't have to hurt us. If I'm not mistaken we'll be long gone the hell out of here before that happens. We weighted the bodies down fairly well. About the only way they'll know for sure what happened to them before sunrise is to send somebody else underwater looking for 'em tonight. I don't see 'em doing that. It's too risky on their part."

She agreed. "True, but so was the attack on the Police Headquarters in Peking. Insanity such as that cannot be confined by logic. Those who do not fear death are the ones we should fear the most."

"Which is why we have to be just as crazy and nasty as they are," Frost mused. "Wackos like them—that's

125

the only kind of treatment they deserve or understand. Sometimes I even think they look forward to it. And where the track records of some of the boys on the other side of this wall are concerned—I'd say we've got our work cut out for us."

"That is, at best, a gross understatement."

"I know that, kid. I'm just trying to cheer ya up."

In silence then they removed their equipment from the weapons bags—Frost first taking out and putting on a pair of ninja-style tabi boots, ankle high with split-toe, and a ridged rubberized sole for traction. Like the uniform he was wearing, the boots were designed for the greatest maximum comfort and freedom of movement—not exactly the sixty-five dollar shoes or combat boots he was used to, but intrinsically practical given the situation.

The tabi boots on, Frost turned his attention to his weapons, beginning with his Comvest shoulder holster with the black checkered rubber Pachmayr-gripped Browning High Power secured inside. Next came the Interdynamics KG-99 semi-automatic assault pistol—Frost easing the sling over his shoulder on the left side. Spare magazines for both the KG-99 and High Power were taken from the bag and inserted below the belt of his uniform. His Gerber MkI boot knife was already in its sheath at the back of the belt.

The final weapon out of Frost's bags was the one Ling had given him on their way to the airstrip beside the Yangtze—the Barnett Commando. Anchoring the fore-end of the Commando against the ground with his left hand and the butt of the bow with his right, Frost pulled back, his knee at the pivot point of the bow's pistol grip, allowing the butt of the stock to pivot, the pivotal motion drawing two cocking levers up and to the rear of the stock, drawing the bow string back into a fully cocked position. Cocking the Commando automatically applied the bow's safety.

Taking the bow's leather quiver from the now-empty weapons bag, and attaching it to his belt with a strip of velcro fastened to the quiver's back, Frost drew a broad-head hunting bolt, placing it in the Commando's flight groove, with the flat base of the shaft flush against the string. A small retaining spring lever held the bolt in place, which meant that the Commando would be ready to fire whenever he was.

Close to finishing emptying her weapons bag, Elizabeth stood and smiled. "A moment more and we can go." She adjusted a utility belt around her waist—this containing pouches filled with grenades, spare magazines for the Type 50M SMG she wore over her shoulder. Then she opened one of the larger pouches for Frost to see. "The Bauer radio transmitter for signaling the helicopter is in here. If you would feel safer carrying it, I will not be offended."

"Then you won't be offended when I tell you that I feel safe knowing the transmitter is in your hands. Besides," Frost laughed, "if I try loading any more on this belt of mine—my pants will fall down."

Getting across the lake to the island undetected had presented one set of problems, getting up and over the walls, another. He had expressed his doubts when hearing Ling's plan for scaling the stronghold's fifty-foot walls. Frost's objections to the plan had been purely personal, based more on a strong dislike for heights, rather than the belief that Ling's plan wouldn't work.

"I couldn't talk you into letting me piggyback-it up the wall with you, could I?" he asked.

"Hank," Elizabeth returned, dipping into her weapons bag for the last pieces of equipment contained inside, "you mustn't be nervous. You'll do just fine.

Now, put these on so we can go."

She then handed him two sets of tekagi—one pair for his hands, the other to be strapped around his knees. The tekagi, which were also known as tiger claws, were hook devices traditionally worn by the ninja on their hands, knees and feet, enabling them to climb sheer walls. Resigned to the fact that Hank Frost, Human Fly, was about to go on, the one-eyed man donned the tekagi without further protest. He'd used similar gear before, but not after a long swim or on a wall of such height.

"There," he said, once they were on, "how do I look?"

"Like a walking can opener."

"Ha, ha. So do you."

"Do you want me to go first so you can see how it's done?"

He shook his head. "Uh uh, we'll do it together. That way it cuts over overall exposure out in the open by half."

"All right, then." She carefully avoided the tekagi on Frost's knees and leaned in to kiss his cheek. "Kung hei fat choy!—It means 'May you be blessed with prosperity,' a Chinese way of saying 'good luck.' I will see you at the top."

"Not if I get there first," he promised, then muttered under his breath, "Fat chance of that."

They made a final check to see that they were leaving nothing of importance behind—all was in order—then stepped from beneath the shelter of the tree, turned, facing the wall, and began to climb . . .

He was halfway up the moonlit wall, feeling at the moment as vulnerable as a bug trapped under a flashlight, and the muscles of his arms and his back were killing him. He settled his weight onto the tekagi binding his knees, braced himself with his left hand, then pulled the tiger claws on his right hand out from the wall and stretched—reaching up as high as he could with his right hand before driving the claws on his hand back into the wall. He repeated the same action with his left hand, and then with both knees, one at a time, scaling the wall as though climbing a ladder, his progress to him seeming excruciatingly slow.

Elizabeth, on the other hand, was having no apparent difficulty at all. She had set the pace at the beginning of the climb, and had not looked back since. Even now, as Frost threw his right hand out and up to lift himself higher, the soles of the woman's tabis were a good two feet over his head.

Frost was in the process of concluding that all they needed was circus music and a contract to take their act on the road. The moon overhead was as bright as a spotlight, and if he tried really hard he could almost imagine the smell of popcorn. The only thing missing was the audience which—given the present choice of spectators available—suited him fine.

He worked his hands and knees against the wall, swinging, digging, shifting and lifting, pulling his way upward, fighting gravity and the strain on his muscles to reach the top. Then Frost tilted his head back and up just as Elizabeth cleared the top of the wall, pulled herself over and disappeared. He clawed his way into the wall, climbing and lifting himself higher, and was preparing to swing his right hand up and out for the last leg of his climb, when a gruff male voice—coming from just over the lip of the wall—halted Frost's motion in midair.

"Ting-shi!" the gruff voice hissed. *"Bu-yao-dong!"*

A guard on duty had obviously caught Elizabeth sneaking over the wall, but for some reason was holding off sounding an alarm. Frost didn't intend giving him the chance.

"Pssst!" Frost made the noise, loud enough for only the guard to hear. "Pssst!"

"*Shen-me?*" the guard said and then his oval, curious face appeared over the rim of the wall, looking down.

"Goodbye," Frost said, swinging his right arm up and over, sinking the tekagi hooks deep into the back of the stunned guard's cranium, crunching through the base of the skull—putting the upward roll of the dying guard's eyes on permanent hold.

"Ahhh," Frost grunted, arching his back and pulling with his right arm, dragging the body over the wall until the dead guard's weight got into the act and did the job for him—wrenching the tiger claws from his hand, and flipping the corpse over the wall in a fall to the rock-strewn beach below.

There was a thud and a snap, followed by a gurgling noise, and then another body came sailing over the wall, dropping toward the body already there.

Then a hand—Elizabeth's—was reachng over the wall, grasping his, helping him the rest of the way up.

"Caught me with my pants down," Frost admitted as he silently lowered his boots into the fortress. "I thought the guard was alone."

"No." Elizabeth shook her head. "There were two of them."

Frost quietly slipped the tekagi from his left hand.

Chapter Eighteen

"What do you think we should do?" she asked.

"Climb back down to the lake and swim for home."

"I'm serious."

"So am I." Frost nodded in the direction of the fortress courtyard three stories below. "Look at 'em. Not counting the ones we can't see—we're talking a good hundred of the enemy force, maybe even double that amount."

"Should we signal for the helicopters?"

Frost shook his head. "Not until we know for sure about Thoresen. No one knows we're in here yet, so we still have some time to play with."

"Until the guards we disposed of over the wall are discovered missing."

"Right," Frost concurred. "Which means we've got to step on it. That building in the center there looks to be the main headquarters in this place. I'm betting that's where we'll find Thoresen."

"Agreed. But how do you suggest we get from Point A to Point B?"

"Getting there is easy. It's getting there without them killing us where it starts to get tricky. The first thing we have to do is get down to the ground." He looked from side to side. "You don't think they have an elevator hiding nearby?"

"No, but there are sure to be some stairs. Of course,"

she added, "we could always climb down with the tekagi."

"Forget that," Frost countered. "We'll take the stairs . . ."

Clinging to the shadows they could find, and hurrying between the open spaces of moonlight when they came to them, Frost and Elizabeth reached the stairwell apparently unobserved since no alarm was sounded, then started down. Prepared for the unexpected, Frost had passed his thumb over the Barnett Commando's safety and was carrying it in an assault position—ready to fire.

While much of the courtyard was illuminated—in addition to the coverage provided by the moon—by several large floodlights which were powered by a gasoline fueled generator they could hear operating in the far northwest corner of the compound—the interior of the enclosed stairwell they were in was swathed in patches of darkness, only occasionally interrupted by the odd bare low-wattage light bulbs strung indiscriminately along the stairs.

There were four flights of stairs leading to the courtyard, and as they successfully made it to the landing of the second floor, the one-eyed man and his female companion breathed a collective sigh of relief. They were rounding the landing and starting down the third flight of stairs when a noise reached Frost's ears—the sound of someone moving on the bottom steps below and starting up.

To try and make a run for it could be a fatal mistake, Frost knew. It could only trap them somewhere on the second or third level, plus there was the danger that the intruder coming up the steps would take notice of their flight and sound the alarm. Another reason backtracking was out of the question was because it wouldn't put them any closer to where Frost believed Thoresen was being held captive. That left only one alternative.

"Bluff it," he rasped to Elizabeth. "Maybe we'll get lucky."

She bobbed her head in agreement as Frost lowered the Commando from its assault position, just as the intruder—a swarthy Chinese with a fat face and a sluggish seeming disposition, lazily toting a Type 56 assault rifle in his hands—rounded the bend in the stairwell and began to climb.

Saying nothing and moving to the side of the darkened stairway to allow the man to pass, Frost and Elizabeth kept walking, their chins tucked low and into their chests to better conceal their faces as the man walked by, not saying a word or giving any other sign of greeting. Frost was ready to celebrate their minor victory with a quiet word to Elizabeth when his fleeting feeling of triumph withered in an instant—the Chinese climbing the stairs had stopped moving.

The guard was already bringing his Type 56 assault rifle into play when Frost reacted—wheeling on his feet, whipping the Commando up at his target, finger twitching on the Barnett's trigger, the seventeen-and-a-half inch bolt and its three-bladed Bear Satellite broadhead snapping from the bow with a muted whoosh of air, jumping across the less than fifteen feet separating bolt from target, and striking the man dead before the muzzle of his rifle got any higher than his knees.

"Ugggh!" the man uttered an inhuman grunt as the Commando's broadhead cut completely through him, digging savagely between two ribs, then exploding out his back with such tremendous force that the hunting bolt lodged in the wall—the aluminum shaft bent and broke just above the broadhead as the body of the dead man sank to the floor.

Frost darted back up the stairs, his immediate concern being the disposal of the body. That no one else was aware of the fatal—and brief—confrontation, Frost was certain. If any others had heard a betraying sound, now the enclosed stairwell would have been filled with enemy troops and they would have been trapped. The very absence of those troops was a positive sign.

Spotting a curtained doorway on the right, some ten feet away from the second floor landing, Frost grabbed the body by the shoulders and pulled, dragging it the short distance to the doorway and shoving the body through. The doorway led to a tiny room, without windows, that was rich with the stink of mildew and neglect, but otherwise empty. It was the perfect place for dumping the dead man.

"This is depressing," Frost commented, cocking the Commando by bringing it across his knee this time, then loading its flight groove with another of the broadhead hunting bolts from the leather quiver at his side. There were eighteen bolts remaining. "We can't keep this up. At the rate we're going we're bumping them off on the average of one every minute. Sooner or later we'll run out of places to hide the bodies—then it really will hit the fan."

"Right—the old crapola," Elizabeth said, prompting Frost to chuckle. "What's so funny?" she asked.

"You and 'the old crapola' bit," Frost answered. "Hardly the language I would expect from such a lovely Chinese lady."

"You are forgetting that I have been formally trained by my government to pass as an American."

"I haven't forgotten," Frost's tone sobered. "I was just trying not to remember. But back to the bodies piling up?"

"That is easy. We must simply strive to be more creative."

134

"Eight stiffs in the last half hour isn't being creative?" Frost asked as they departed from the room and started back down the stairs. "How do you suggest we spiff up our act?"

"By keeping a lower profile, not killing anyone unless absolutely necessary, and if we do have to kill, then we must make certain that disposal facilities for the bodies are close at hand."

"That's guerilla warfare by a poorly written textbook—it hardly applies to our situation here and now."

"I know that," Elizabeth said, her hand reaching out and giving his arm a friendly squeeze. "I'm just giving you more of that old crapola."

"Wonderful," Frost gritted his teeth as they came to the bottom of the stairs and the threshold to the fortress courtyard.

Chapter Nineteen

As they had done while still on the wall, Frost and Elizabeth hugged their bodies to the pockets of darkness when they could find them, quickly skirting along the edges of the lighted patches when they could not—beginning their hazardous trek from one side of the fortress to the other—making for the elegant appearing tri-storied structure which dominated all else in the courtyard.

From their starting point at the bottom of the stairwell leading down from the wall, Frost had an excellent view of the assorted buildings housed within the fortress. To his immediate left, seventy yards down, adjacent to the south wall and the main gate, was the company mess hall. Even as Frost watched, a long line of the pro-Soviet terrorists could be seen filing into the hall to receive their evening meal, and while it was true that not so much as a slight breeze was stirring the air that night, the aromatic smells spilling from the kitchen—cooking rice, fish and vegetables—still found their way to Frost, making the one-eyed man's mouth water.

Traveling away from the mess hall, moving south to west, were a barracks compound, latrine, and armory, followed by a wide open space that was half the length of a football field. A small building bordered the field to the right—possibly an infirmary—then there was another barracks, and finally the focal point of the courtyard, the three-story complex Frost and the woman were trying to reach.

Suspended on posts the size of telephone poles, and situated next to each of the barracks, were the flood-lights Frost had seen earlier. These, combined with the silvery glare reflecting off the moon, gave the interior of the fortress a blanched quality of stark illumination.

I thought I ordered clouds? Frost mused as they made it to the eastern corner of the barracks building next to the infirmary. If it hadn't been for the fact that most of the terrorists were occupied with having dinner, the corner of the barracks would have been the last place to stage the final assault on their main target. As it was no out of the ordinary noises could be heard coming from inside the barracks, only the scratchy melody of an old phonograph record.

Frost peered around the corner of the barracks building at their primary objective. The three-story structure stood approximately thirty yards from the barracks and was supported by a foundation of harsh granite blocks—great pieces of stone jutting from the foundation like a row of ugly teeth. A steep narrow column of steps—also of stone—bisected the foundation, climbing to a single door which opened to the building inside. Two armed guards, seeming more alert than the man they had killed in the stairwell, were positioned at attention in front of the door, barring the entrance to all unauthorized intruders.

"How come they're not eating with everyone else?" Frost whispered.

"They probably had their dinner before coming on duty," Elizabeth replied. "Or maybe someone brings supper to them later."

"Yeah, well whatever the case, we have to get by

137

them. Although there probably is another way into the building, it would cost us too much valuable time trying to find it. And with those guys we took care of bound to be missed—especially during chow—that's something we can't afford. Like it or not we've gotta go through those guards."

"Any ideas?" Elizabeth wondered.

Frost paused as the phonograph record stopped and then started playing again. "How about if I yell 'charge' and let you lead the attack?"

The woman closed her right fist and pointed her thumb to the ground. "No tickee-no washee on that one, Hank."

"Okay, no sweat, I gotta another idea, but you're not going to like it any better."

"Try me."

Frost did and he was right—Elizabeth didn't like the idea. But they decided to go with it anyway.

Frost knew the real secret behind successful role camouflage was the ability to blend in with your surroundings, to make those you are attempting to deceive truly believe that you belong in the role you are playing. That was precisely what Elizabeth was trying to accomplish as she left the shadowed space she had been sharing with Frost, crossed the thirty yards separating the barracks from their three-storied objective, and climbed the narrow column of steps leading to the building's entrance like it was something she did every day of the week. Which was how—Frost hoped—it would look if any of the guards, posted in the towers in each corner of the fortress, happened to notice her walking across the courtyard.

Moving with a natural stride that totally belied what she must have been feeling inside, Frost held his breath as Elizabeth reached the top of the stone steps, casually advancing toward the pair of armed guards stationed there. Frost chose that moment to raise the Commando crossbow to his shoulder and sight through the 4 x 32mm scope at the scene taking place, carefully leading the target—because what he would be aiming at was less than fifty yards away—so that the point of impact would be slightly higher than where the reticle indicated. He whisked his thumb over the extruding button at the receiver rear, releasing the safety. His target was—the terrorist standing watch to the right of the doorway.

As Elizabeth approached the men Frost could see the expression on his target's face go from simple curiosity, to surprise, and finally to anger. The guard said something to her, but even if the man had been speaking to Elizabeth in English, the noise coming from the power generator operating behind the building would have prevented the words from being intelligible to him. But no matter. With what was taking place at the moment, knowledge of what was being said was unnecessary. The guard's physical actions told the story.

That the guards had not threatened Elizabeth with their weapons as she approached was a good sign, telling Frost that the various factions assembled within the stronghold had not been together long enough for the guards to recognize Elizabeth as a stranger. The fact that they were conversing with her told the one-eyed man something else, too. Although they hadn't encountered any yet, some of the terrorists participating in the campaign to wring a confession from the American emissary had to be women.

The guard framed in Frost's scope shook his head back and forth, then pointed with his finger—the gesture clearly ordering Elizabeth to retrace her steps and to vacate the restricted area immediately. Following the instructions Frost had given her, Elizabeth nodded to the guard on her left—two feet in front of her—that she was taking their advice and leaving. Then she started turning away to the right.

Which was when Frost fired, working his finger against the Commando's trigger, feeling no recoil, only a slight pulling forward, hearing a subtle whoosh and a twang, and the 175-pound draw was expended—launching the three-bladed broadhead into the air and straight at the heart of his target.

Even as the dead-on-his feet terrorist was starting to collapse and Frost was lowering and reloading his cross-bow, he saw Elizabeth was swinging into action—pivoting in a flash back to her left, the knife held in her right fist pounding into the chest of the second guard, killing the man before he had the chance to cry out.

Frost's heart felt like it wanted to burst as he left the protection of the barracks' eastern side and began crossing the ninety-odd feet to Elizabeth. He was one hundred percent vulnerable now. If any of the guards in the towers had been watching, this was when they would strike, cutting him down with a sniper shot to the back. He reached the narrow stairway and began to climb—his mind picturing the crosshairs of a scope lining up on his head. They were toying with him, fooling him into thinking that . . . But then he was next to Elizabeth. Still standing. Still alive—the imagined sniper in his mind evaporating in a sigh of relief.

"Nice going," he commented to the woman.

"Good shooting," she returned, supporting the dead weight of the guard she had stabbed. "By now we should have this routine down pretty well. Shall we?"

"We shall."

Doing their best to make it appear "normal" that they should be removing the bodies of the dead guards from the entrance to the building, Frost and Elizabeth dragged the terrorists through the doorway and out of sight, depositing the bodies down an open chute cut from the wall and which led to a cellar and which would have, Elizabeth explained, originally been used for the disposal of garbage.

"Same difference," Frost remarked upon hearing the explanation. "Trash is trash is trash."

"We must hurry."

"I know," he said as they rushed along a low-ceilinged hallway, checking any rooms they came to as they passed, finding all of them empty. "We've been lucky with other terrs we took out. No one's noticed they're A.W.O.L. yet. But that's not gonna be the case with the pair we shot down the chute. I give us five minutes tops, and then this place is going to be crawling with unfriendlies."

They reached the end of the deserted corridor without seeing anyone or anything worth noting—except for a set of stairs going up, which they took, climbing the steps two at a time, their rubber-soled tabi boots carrying them upward in silence.

A fast but intensive search of the second floor produced nothing of value. There were signs that some of the rooms they checked out were being utilized as living quarters, but the occupants in question were either out to chow, or else upstairs doing whatever it was they were doing on the third floor.

Which Frost was determined to find out as they ran up the last flight of stairs to investigate.

Where the stairway opening onto the second floor had done so onto a low-ceilinged hallway like the one of the first level, when Frost and Elizabeth came to the top of the last flight of stairs it was to discover a short corridor—fifteen feet long—leading to a narrow chamber that was as wide as the overall building itself.

There were no windows in the oddly proportioned room—only a dark metal door directly across from where they were standing.

Frost lifted his right foot to step into the room as Elizabeth suddenly yanked on his arm—pulling him back. At first he didn't understand her actions, but once he took a hard look at the interior of the strange narrow room, the reason why Elizabeth had stopped him was clear.

From one end of the room to the other—with the exception of a twelve-inch strip fronting the opposite wall—the floor was covered with an intricate lattice-work of thin bamboo laced together with vines. Frost didn't know the Chinese name for what he was looking at, but in Japan such exotic methods of wall-to-wall carpeting were referred to as cricket floors—a floor specifically designed to emit loud noises when anyone walked on it. If Elizabeth hadn't stopped him the racket resulting from his walking across the floor would have been loud enough for the guards posted behind the door opposite to hear.

Frost gauged the distance across the wide and narrow room—maybe twenty feet—vastly too far to clear with a jump even with a good run to back it up. Doubly frustrating because Frost's instinct told him that Bruce Thoresen was somewhere on the other side of the metal door. The American had to be there. The short hallway they were in and the odd room they were facing hardly contained a fraction of the third floor's available space. Also, if Thoresen wasn't on the third floor, then why go to all the trouble of installing a metal security door in the first place? No, Thoresen was somewhere very nearby, all right, and they had to get to him.

Frost checked the face of his Rolex. Close to five minutes had elapsed since they had entered the building. Too long.

"It's times like this when I wish I'd been born with wings," Frost said. "About the only way to get from here to the other side of the room is to fly."

"We will not have to fly," Elizabeth matter-of-factly stated. "We can cross along the ceiling."

"With what? We got rid of those tiger claws we were using while we were still on the wall."

The woman shook her head. "We will not need the tekagi." She snapped open two of the larger pouches on her utility belt. "I have something else we can use."

"How the hell did you know to bring those?"

She smiled. "I am trained to be prepared. Now, we must hurry. Put these on."

And with that she passed Frost the climbing gear—four massive suction cups like the kind wing walkers would use. Frost took the devices from her and remarked, "How did you know what size to get me?"

"One size fits all—now hurry!"

Following Elizabeth's example, Frost attached the large suctions cups to his body—one strapped to each knee, the others fastened to his hands—wearing them much the same as he had worn the tekagi, but with a smooth concave surface on the inside instead of hooks.

"All set," he announced. "If we get out of this in one piece, remind me to send you the doctor's bill for treating my aching back."

"It's not that far across the room. You will be fine."

"Try telling that to my back . . ."

As agile as ever, Elizabeth moved up the side of the wall and to a polished oak beam which traversed the ceiling from above the beginning of the cricket floor, all the way across the room to where the black metal door was waiting to be opened. Not to be outdone, Frost soon started up the wall, too—awkwardly climbing as best he could to keep up with Elizabeth, ever aware that a single false move could send him tumbling with a crash to the cricket floor.

Transferring from the wall to the wide oak beam was an arduous task, but by working the suction cups carefully, one at a time, he was eventually able to trade the relative comfort of the vertical wall for the horizontal hell of the beam.

"Shit," Frost muttered as he held onto the beam, above the floor twenty-five feet below, hanging upside down like a sloth clinging to a tree branch. The Barnett Commando and the Interdynamics KG-99 had both slipped around on their respective slings and were dangling underneath—the muscles in his shoulders and lower back were screaming at him for the torture he was putting them through.

"Are you okay?" Elizabeth whispered from ahead.

"Wonderful," he whispered his reply. "Just wonderful."

He worked the suction cup on his right hand loose in preparation of moving further along the beam, when the suction cup holding his left hand in place suddenly lost pressure and broke free, too. Unable to prevent it, Frost started to drop, gravity pulling his shoulders and head in a crash dive to the floor, the one-eyed man expecting, at the very least, a broken neck. But instead of falling to the floor, Frost's body was wrenched with a violent jolt as his knees—still attached to the oaken beam with suction cups of their own—found themselves supporting all of his weight and that of his weapons.

Blood rushed to his head and floaters danced across his eye as he swayed back and forth, his topsy-turvy view of the world making him dizzy and sick to his stomach. He closed his eye and took several deep breaths, waiting for the swinging and sensation of nausea to cease.

Finally—after he sensed he wasn't moving any more, and also that his supper of whatever it was that Ling had dished up was going to stay put—Frost opened his eye.

"This will never do," Elizabeth's hushed words came at him as she hurried back along the beam to his aid. "Are you hurt?"

"Only my pride."

"Can you swing back up to the beam?"

"If I didn't have all this equipment hanging from me—sure." He tried raising his body, only managing to pull himself up several inches before having to drop back again. "Damn, I'm not going anywhere."

Elizabeth moved further along, closer to where his knees were suction-cupped to the beam. "I'm going to try to lift you up with my gun."

"Forget it. Try that and we'll have both of us dangling from the ceiling."

But Elizabeth was already following through with her plan—releasing her right hand from the beam, holding the K-50M SMG in the crook of her arm, while bracing its stock against her side, then leaning over so that the Type 50's muzzle was about a foot above his face. "Can you reach it?"

Frost, flicking his eye to the ceiling, grumbled. "I sure hope ya got the safety on." He swung his arms beneath him in a rocking motion to get his body swinging back and forth again, then rapidly inhaled as he brought his arms over and up, attempting to curl his wrists around the end of Elizabeth's gun. Somehow he made it, wrapping his wrists about the SMG's muzzle, unable to properly grasp it because of the suction cups still attached to his hands.

"Good," Elizabeth voiced a whispered word of encouragement for them both as Frost began slowly climbing back up to the ceiling and the oaken beam as the

145

woman steadied the gun. His stomach muscles felt like the neighborhood punching bag, but he was doing it. A couple more inches and he would be . . .

"No!" Frost hissed and, even as he spoke, the Bauer radio transmitter was slipping from its pouch in Elizabeth's utility belt. The flap on the pouch had fallen open and, with it, the fabric barrier that was holding the transmitter secure. As the transmitter cleared the inverted pouch and dropped—Frost did also—simultaneously relinquishing his grip on the Type 50, throwing his arms out, clapping his hands together, pinning the transmitter between them, and keeping them clasped together as he once more found himself hanging upside down. Deja-vu, Frost thought, then muttered, "Shit."

Working his cupped-together hands around and up so that they were positioned near his waist, the one-eyed man delicately eased the Bauer transmitter from between his palms and into the waistband of his ninja-style garment. He removed his hands and the transmitter stayed in place, then he started swinging his body again, going back and forth enough to be able to reach the muzzle of Elizabeth's K-50M. This time when he neared the oak beam he was successful in his attempt to get his hands re-attached. He allowed air to escape slowly between his lips as Elizabeth continued along the beam again, and he began to follow. Ninety seconds later he was back on his somewhat wobbly feet, standing upon the foot-wide strip of the tile adjacent to the cricket floor.

Quickly they removed and packed away the suction cups from their hands and knees, enjoying their moment of triumph. They had crossed the room in silence without alerting any of the enemy. Frost's flicker of elation died a fast death, though, as he tested the black metal door and found it was locked.

"This just isn't my day," Frost decided, wondering what to do next when Elizabeth tapped him on the shoulder, holding up several objects for him to see. The one-eyed man grinned. They were facing a locked door, but Elizabeth had the key to open it—a half ounce of C-3 plastique explosive.

Consisting of 77% RDK, 3% tetryl, 4%TNT, and 6% Plastisize-Cotton-Nitro—C-3 was the best locksmith in the world when it came to opening obstinate doors. And as Elizabeth packed the plastique around a large hinge near the top of the door, Frost withdrew the transmitter from the waistband of his uniform and activated the signal that would alert the helicopter force to start in; his feeling being that, once the C-3 was detonated, they were going to need all the help they could get.

Elizabeth wired the plastique with a small electric detonator powered by four AA batteries, setting the timer for sixty seconds, then rushing with Frost along the bare strip of tile as far away from the metal door as possible—Frost feeling cheated because the precarious climb across the ceiling had been a total waste of time.

"If they didn't know we were here before," he said, "they sure as hell will now."

And Frost was right.

147

Chapter Twenty

The force of the explosion rocked the long narrow room they were in like a card table struck by an earthquake, its shockwave rolling across the room, riddling the walls with inch-wide fissures, cracking away part of the broad oak beam, and reducing the once-menacing cricket floor to a forest of toothpicks as Frost and Elizabeth—fingers plugging their ears and screaming as loud as they could—waited for the thunder of the blast to subside.

The air was still swirling with debris when Frost, letting the Commando crossbow hang at his side, brought the KG-99 forward on its sling, working the bolt and chambering a round, then tapped Elizabeth firmly on the shoulder and shouted, "Let's go!"

Frost was up and running—the woman close behind—charging down the bare strip of tile on the floor for the jagged gash of twisted metal that had been the door. Smoke and dust and the sounds of pained confusion were spewing through the open hole as Frost, accepting one of the grenades from Elizabeth's utility belt, gripped the safety lever, tugged on the pull ring, and then lobbed the grenade around the corner and through the open doorway.

The concussion of the explosion shook the wall they were leaning against, followed by horrified screams of terrorists learning to die. Some of the smoke cleared and Frost had to grit his teeth in disgust at the sight at his feet—the severed black-clad forearm of a Night Ghost, its hand still gripping one of the deadly Cern Do broadswords.

"Ready?" Frost looked to his partner.

"Ready," Elizabeth returned.

"Now!"

Holding the KG-99 at the ready, Frost carefully dove through the gnarled wreckage of the door, finding himself in a wide corridor stretching approximately seventy-five feet before him. To his immediate left and right were the grisly remains of two terrorists. Both had evidently been stationed on the opposite side of the door when the C-3 was detonated and were covered top to bottom with razored pieces of the decimated door. A few steps further showed him the body of the Night Ghost with its missing arm.

"Aaaiiieee!" the crazed cry came at them from one of the many rooms branching off the corridor as a sword-wielding Night Ghost suddenly appeared, howling a string of words Frost couldn't understand, rushing at them down the hallway.

Frost held his ground and opened fire with the KG-99, finger flexing on its trigger, the pistol bucking in his hands, sending a trio of 9mm 115-grain JHPs plowing into this target's chest—the Night Ghost tripping on his own dying feet as he tumbled in death to the floor.

More screams then—from many voices—came echoing along the corridor.

"It's not good, Hank."

"What the hell?"

"They know who we are," Elizabeth explained. "When the Night Ghost you just killed saw us he shouted to his brothers that the 'one-eyed dog' had come to challenge them again. They are screaming all at once like that to frighten us."

"And doing a damn good job of it, too."

Then the screams of the Night Ghosts gained in volume as more than a dozen of the black-garbed fanatics surged into the hallway, each of the shrieking Invisible Ones seeming to Frost to be fighting for position at the head of the line, eager for the honor of slaying him.

But the one-eyed "dog" had other ideas.

Calling for Elizabeth to stand at his side, together Frost and the woman unleashed their weapons on the advancing mob—Frost spraying the Night Ghosts with a hail of bullets from the KG-99, Elizabeth firing the K-50M SMG. Bodies flipped and fell to the floor as the first wave of the attack was eliminated, but the Night Ghosts kept coming, screaming at the top of their lungs, apparently oblivious to the barrage of gunfire striking them down. And despite all of the Night Ghosts who had fallen, they still appeared to be pouring out of the woodwork.

The attacking Night Ghosts were still twenty yards away when a well-aimed shuriken throwing star nearly succeeded in taking Frost's right ear off. Another of the shuriken—this one shaped like a wheel—tore at the fabric of his uniform just under his arm.

Which was when the stick on the KG-99 ran dry.

With no time to reload, and with Elizabeth still snapping away with her K-50M, Frost let the Interdynamics assault pistol drop to his side as he reached for the Barnett Commando, swinging it around, picking his target, and firing—the triple-bladed Bear Satellite broadhead flying from the crossbow, catching one of the Night Ghosts with a geyser shot to the throat, then stabbing into the face of the black-clad figure behind him—both victims dead before they took another step.

The Commando empty, Frost was grabbing for the Metalified Browning High Power, when Elizabeth suddenly stopped firing and threw one of her frag grenades into the center of the Night Ghost mob. Instinctively, Frost and the woman pancaked themselves to the floor and covered their heads and faces as the grenade went off, shards of deadly shrapnel from the explosion adding to the growing toll of dead and dying Night Ghosts.

Then Frost was back on his feet, the Browning High Power out of its Cobra shoulder holster, gripped tightly in his right fist, the one-eyed man thumbing back the hammer, triggering a two-round burst into the heart of the only remaining Night Ghost to have survived the blast from the grenade. The Night Ghost—whose arm had been raised to throw a particularly large shuriken—grunted in apparent surprise at being hit, squeezing his hand hard around the shuriken, fingers clenching the bladed star, slicing two of the digits off. His legs crumbled beneath him and he was dead.

And so were all of the other Night Ghosts as far as Frost could tell.

"Come on!" he shouted to Elizabeth, and then they were running along, jumping over the mass of bodies scattered about the floor, cautiously checking out each of the rooms off the corridor, finding them empty, anxiously making their way to a big metal door at the end of the hallway—an exact duplicate of the one they had destroyed with the C-3.

"Have you got any more of the plastique?" Frost asked.

The woman shook her head.

"We'll use a couple of the grenades, then," he continued, praying in the back of his mind that the helicopter backup he'd signaled for was well on its way as he took the grenade from Elizabeth. "I'll go in first once the door is blown. Stay low and careful what you shoot at. Thoresen's probably in there and we don't want to be hitting him by accident."

Elizabeth nodded that she understood, then together they pulled the pins on their grenades, rolled the pair of them at the black metal door, while simultaneously diving for cover into one of the rooms off to the side. Seconds later the corridor rang with the power of the dual explosions, the force of the twin grenades completely shattering the barrier of the black metal door as Frost looked up.

Frost was preparing to leap back into the hallway when a fresh blast erupted along the corridor, quickly followed by the sharp crackle of flames. The grenades had cut into some sort of fuel line and the building was on fire.

"Damn," Frost muttered, hesitating to see if there were to be any more explosions, deciding there weren't, then charging from the room and into the hallway, the Browning High Power clamped in his right fist as he dove through the hole where the metal door had been.

Flames licked near his shoulders as Frost's right eye scanned the room in an instant, seeing everything, missing nothing. Off to the left were a pair of terrorists, male and female. To his right—an operating table upon which a man, who could only have been Bruce Thoresen, was strapped. Next to Thoresen was a monster wearing a lab coat, desperately trying to fill a hypodermic syringe with the colorless liquid from a vial.

The terrorists would have to go first.

As the terrs raised their rifles—both of the Type 56 assault variety—Frost and Elizabeth beat them to the punch, Elizabeth emptying the last of her thirty-five round 7.62mm magazine into the gut of the male Sovietsympathizer, while a three-shot burst from Frost's High Power punched down the female terrorist.

Frost caught the movement out of the corner of his eye and wheeled, bringing the Browning into play, squeezing off another three shots—each of the 9mm JHPs striking the lab-coated sadist as he lowered the filled hypodermic to Thoresen's arm. Splotches of red mushroomed on the lab coat as the hypo sailed through the air, and the "doctor" who had been holding it slumped to the floor in a pool of his own blood.

"Wha ... ?" Thoresen tried raising his head.

"Easy, fella—we're friends," Frost told him, returning the High Power to his Cobra rig, then taking out the Gerber MkI knife from its sheath at the small of his back and cutting away the straps binding the American to the table. Frost resheathed the blade, then replenished the spent stick in the KG-99, loaded the Commando with another broadhead bolt, and finally replaced the partially-empty magazine in the Browning High Power with a fresh one. Elizabeth was finishing reloading the K-50M with a new thirty-five round magazine as Frost turned to Thoresen and helped the man sit up. "Think you can walk?" he asked.

But instead of answering, all Thoresen did was start to cry, the combination of shock, fatigue, torture and whatever else he had endured over the past three days getting the best of him. "I didn't really want to tell them," he wept. "Not really ... but the ... they made me ... they wouldn't stop unless I ... unless I did what they ..."

"Thoresen!" Frost shouted, trying to force his way through the haze of uncertainty clouding Thoresen's face. "Listen to me. You're gonna have to pull yourself together. We're here to help you, but we can't do that unless you help us, too." He shook the American hard as Thoresen began nodding off. "Damnit, Thoresen—wake up!"

"What?" the American blinked his eyes open, finally awake and listening.

"We have to make a break for it," Frost said.

Thoresen swallowed and looked about the room. "Where is everybody else?"

"You're looking at 'em," Frost snarled. "Now, do ya think you can walk or not?"

"Yeah," Thoresen said. "At least I hope so."

Frost grumbled and confessed, "That makes two of us . . ."

Chapter Twenty-one

The flames had spread to the passageway, eating at the walls and the ceiling, filling the smoldering tunnel with blistering heat and blinding, lung-burning smoke. It was the last place in the world Frost would have chosen to beat his record for the hundred yard dash, but here he was—rushing back down the hallway for the long narrow room with the blown-apart cricket floor, then down the short corridor to the stairway on the opposite side.

Having to do it while supporting most of Bruce Thoresen's weight made the task nearly impossible. It had become clear as soon as Thoresen's feet had touched the floor that, in his weakened state, he was not going to be able to make a run for it unassisted. Grateful, at least, that Thoresen could stand, Frost had the American throw his right arm around his left shoulder, and then they were off, hurrying down the passageway, trying to escape the likely prospect of a fiery grave.

Half-carrying, half-dragging Thoresen beside him, and with Elizabeth helping to clear a path before them, Frost had covered less than twenty-five feet when Thoresen's legs buckled beneath him and the dazed and stunned American passed out.

"Hank!" Elizabeth cried, but Frost waved her on.

"I've got him!" he hollered, then bent and lifted the unconscious Thoresen over his left shoulder and began to run, moving as fast as he could, carefully avoiding some of the bodies of the dead Night Ghosts which were already starting to burn, the sweet-sick stench of roasting flesh assaulting his senses. Then he was past the bodies and in open hallway, his legs pumping like pistons to keep him and his burden upright. He reached the doorway destroyed by the Composition-3 and hurried through, chasing after Elizabeth's fleeting form, part-running, part-stumbling across the long narrow room, emerging out of breath to the short corridor outside.

Shots then—from Elizabeth's SMG—a single three-round burst, quickly followed by another, then silence.

"Hank, hurry!" the woman waved her hand in the air for him to continue.

"What was all the shooting?" Frost asked as he ran to join her.

"Curiosity seekers," was all she said, and then she was gone, disappearing down the stairway—Frost, carrying Thoresen, bringing up the rear.

As the one-eyed man made his way down the steps he was forced to shift to the left to avoid tripping over the 'curiosity seekers' Elizabeth had taken out. The terrorists, both male, had taken hits to the face and chest, and were still twitching spasmodically in the final throes of death. More gunfire from Elizabeth's K-50M sounded from below, with a pair of shots from a smaller caliber weapon answering in return. The woman's SMG roared to life again, there was a scream, and then Elizabeth's face appeared at the landing on the second floor.

"I'm coming, I'm coming," Frost told her, and then he was standing on the landing, too. "More curiosity seekers?"

"Not any more," she smiled.

There was a crashing noise from above, telling Frost that some of the fire-damaged roof had already caved in. Smoke was beginning to funnel down the stairwell, stinging his eye, making him cough.

"It's getting bad," he said, wiping at his eye with his free hand. "Another few minutes and this whole building is gonna look like the middle of a bonfire."

"Just one more floor and then we're out."

"Yeah," Frost agreed as they started down the stairs once more. "Out of the fire and into the frying pan . . ."

By the time they made it to the first floor, Frost's knees were feeling like lumps of warm taffy, the continual strain of Thoresen's additional weight taking its toll on his endurance. It wasn't that Thoresen was that big a man, or that he weighed so much—he wasn't and he didn't—but after a while, and under the wrong conditions, any load could become a heavy one.

They were leaving the stairway, turning to the left and moving along the low-ceilinged corridor that would take them outside. Frost was breathing roughly, his body screaming at him to call time out, when something changed—the six pro-Soviet terrorists who materialized all at once in the doorway ahead.

Not wanting to, but powerless to prevent it, Frost lowered Thoresen to the floor in a dropping roll—catching the back of the unconscious American's head before it could smack the ground—then fell to the right with the Interdynamics KG-99 barking in his hands. Once, twice, three times his finger jerked back on the trigger, its clean six-pound letoff spitting a web of fury into the faces of the onrushing madmen. Two of the terrorists "died for the cause" with prefrontal lobotomies, a third shrieking fanatic caught one of the 115-grain metal jacketed hollow points in his mouth.

Elizabeth dispatched two more of the men, lacing one open from sternum to crotch, then shooting another apart with a burst over the heart; both bodies flopped to the floor.

Frost and Elizabeth were zeroing in on the sixth and

157

final terrorist when the gunman threw his assault rifle into the air and dove—headfirst—into the chute leading to the cellar.

"Damn," the woman swore in English. "He got away."

"Nah," Frost disagreed, easing the KG-99 to his side, then crossing to heft Bruce Thoresen's weight back on his shoulder. "How far would you guess it is down to the cellar?"

"From here—thirty, maybe forty feet. Why?"

"Our boy didn't get away, then. The fall probably killed him and, if it didn't, he'll cook when the building burns to its foundations. And from the looks of things, that won't be long." He glanced behind him to where smoke from the fire raging upstairs was beginning to pour from the stairwell and into the confined space of the corridor they were in.

Wrapping his left arm around the back of Thoresen's legs to hold the American in place, Frost pushed his way down the passage with Elizabeth, reaching its end and stopping where the doorway opened onto the fortress courtyard. With Elizabeth's aid he gently lowered Thoresen to the floor, then turned to see what was happening outside, cautiously peering around the corner of the doorway.

Three bullets tore away pieces of the doorjamb near his face as Frost pulled his head back into the corridor and out of range.

"Well," Frost reported with a sigh, "at least we know they know we're here." He shrugged. "I don't suppose there's another way out of here?"

"There's always the chute," Elizabeth said.

"Ha, ha. No, even if there is another way out, we'd have to go back down the hallway to get to it. And the way it's filling up with the smoke, going back in that direction is out of the question."

"Do you think they'll try to rush us?"

"Uh uh. No need to. All they have to do is keep us where we are for us to end up roasting alive."

"That doesn't sound like much fun."

"Well, you speak the language—you tell 'em that. Tell 'em that they've made a big mistake and that if they let us walk out of here, we'll call it square with each other in all corners. What do you think?" Her reply consisted of a sour frown. "Yeah, that's what I thought."

"I have no desire to perish in the flames."

"Neither do I, kid."

"Which is why I have decided that, if I must perish, then it shall be on the battlefield facing my enemy. It is what I am trained to do. I will not stay here while the building burns down around me."

"You're thinking of making a run for it? You'd be lucky to get ten feet."

"And yet it is better than waiting for the fire."

Frost consulted the face of his Rolex. "Speaking of waiting—where the hell are the helicopters? They should have been here by now."

"Maybe the signal we sent out did not get through," she offered, coming to him, throwing her arms around his neck, kissing him hard on the mouth, pressing her lips to his, then quickly drawing away. "Goodbye, Hank Frost. I am sorry now that when we walked from our camp last night that you did not let me drop my blanket. Goodbye."

"Wait! Elizabeth."

"No!"

The woman gripped the wire stock of her K-50M SMG with her right hand, supporting the weight of the handguard with her left. She looked back briefly to Frost once again, then started out the doorway.

"Elizabeth!" Frost jumped to his feet and grabbed the woman from behind as waves of gunfire erupted from the courtyard, starting off with several scattered shots, then abruptly exploding.

"They are attacking?" she asked.

"No, Elizabeth—we are!"

And then over the barrage of the terrorists' gunfire they heard it—the air-chopping of the approaching helicopter force. Frost carefully stepped to the doorway, venturing to take another look outside, his action drawing none of the enemy's fire as before. The fortress courtyard was a perfect model of pandemonium. Terrorists, sprinkled with the odd Night Ghost he could see, were scurrying about like ants on a hotplate, jockeying for a position of strength as the five helicopters loomed into view.

There was a crashing noise from above them as more of the building caved in on itself, and a hasty examination to his rear showed Frost through the smoke that the flames had reached the bottom of the steps. He went to Thoresen's still unconscious form, bent over and lifted the man to his left shoulder, then turned to Elizabeth, saying, "It's getting too hot for us in here. Let's go."

Elizabeth could only smile in response as they made their exit from the growing inferno inside the building, Frost holding Thoresen with one hand, his KG-99 with the other. By now two of the helicopters had their sliding doors open and were hovering above the expansive field between the infirmary and the armory, the commandos inside the choppers preparing to rappel into battle as drop lines were lowered from the 'copters to the ground. Immediately, the first of the commandos appeared rappelling down the line, then another and another, until the lines running from the helicopters to the field below seemed to be covered with a constant stream of men.

As they descended the lines the commandos were

blatantly vulnerable—some of them taking hits from enemy bullets while still above the field—but for the balance of the rappelling exercise the pro-Soviet attack on the commandos was kept to a minimum, strafing fire coming from one of the other helicopters.

What Frost could see, though, as he and Elizabeth approached the narrow row of steps leading to the courtyard and the first of the barracks buildings, was that the gunship's life could be measured in seconds if the terrorist stationed in the guard tower in the far right hand corner of the fortress had his way.

The terrorist was manning what looked from a distance to be a simple telescope mounted on a tripod. What the plain-in-appearance weapon actually was, Frost realized, had nothing to do with star gazing. It was a Chicom Type 52 recoilless rifle—likely armed with a 75mm HE shell that had a maximum range of 7,300 yards. At the distance the terr was going for—less than fifty yards—it would be impossible to miss. One hit from the Type 52 would blow the chopper out of the sky.

Whispering an apology to Thoresen that the unconscious American couldn't hear, Frost lowered the man to the ground once more, taking up the Barnett Commando crossbow, getting his sighting on the terrorist in the tower adjusted through the Commando's 4 x 32mm light gathering scope, releasing the safety with a brush of his thumb, then moving his finger against the trigger and wishing off—keeping his scope trained on his target's face.

One heartbeat the terrorist was lining up his sights on the hovering gunship, the next he was dead and wearing a Bear Satellite broadhead hunting bolt through his ribcage. The terrorist's body slumped over the end of the Type 52 and remained upright.

Frost quickly reloaded the Commando as the heavy barrage of gunfire continued.

"Normally," Frost cracked, "the last thing I'd expect to cheer me up would be five helicopters full of Chinese Communist commandos. Still, it just goes to show what kind of day it's been." He licked his lips, wishing he had a cigarette. "I don't imagine one of the choppers is going to fly over here and pick us up, so I guess that means we're going to have to get down there and go to them."

"Let me carry the American, then," the woman volunteered. "You must be exhausted."

"Forget it. He's too heavy for you."

"Nonsense. Part of my physical training to become an operative consisted of having to carry bags of rice, equally as heavy as Mr. Thoresen, more than a mile."

"Very impressive, but no cigar." Frost wearily hefted Thoresen onto his left shoulder again, doing his best to make it appear easier than it actually was. "I've carried Thoresen this far—I can do it the rest of the way."

"You're a stubborn man, Hank Frost."

"And you, Elizabeth Chu'an, are too beautiful a woman to be in this business."

She grinned at the compliment. "That's a very chauvinistic attitude."

Frost agreed, "Damn right it is . . ."

They had reached the barracks and were making for the infirmary when four terrorists, apparently fleeing from the attacking commandos, rounded the corner of the small medical facility—running straight for them, their faces lit by the flames of the burning headquarters building behind. Initially, Frost guessed, the terrorists mistook him and Elizabeth for a couple of Night Ghosts, but by the time they realized the error, it was too late.

Frost's trigger finger pumped the KG-99, burning out half the magazine as hot brass from Elizabeth's weapon pelted the skin of his face and neck, the four terrorists going down.

162

Frost paused only long enough to redistribute Thoresen's weight, then hurried with Elizabeth, moving at the fastest pace he could manage, toward the infirmary. The din from the conflict within the fortress was deafening. The sounds of battle were everywhere and the screams of those dying from mortal wounds were impossible to ignore. Smoke and cordite filled the air, turning the silvery coin of the moon into a dull white blur.

Frost and Elizabeth made it to the infirmary, the one-eyed man moving down the right side of the building to where he could risk a glance around the structure's corner at the activity on the open field. Two of the helicopters had pulled up and away after the commandos they had transported had rappelled into the fortress. Two more choppers had landed on the field, while the gunship hovering overhead was still providing a line of cover fire for the commando force on the ground.

As Frost watched he could see O'Hara—framed in the open cabin doorway of one of the helicopters on the ground—emerging into the fight. O'Hara was wielding the Heckler & Koch G-11 caseless gun Ling had given him, blasting away at the pro-Soviet reactionaries.

"Frost!" O'Hara's booming voice bellowed across the length of the open field just as Ling jumped from the helicopter's cabin to battle alongside the man from the FBI. "Frost—get your ass over here!"

The one-eyed man took a deep breath and nodded to Elizabeth. "What a pest!"

And then they were running, leaving the relative safety and shelter of the infirmary building, charging across the open space of the field to where O'Hara and the two choppers were waiting.

"O'Hara!" Frost shouted, his legs pumping beneath him, carrying him and Thoresen in a headlong rush over the field. "O'Hara!"

"Frost!" the one-eyed man's friend shouted back in

response, swinging his H&K G-11 around to cover their flight. "Come on, sport—you can make it!"

Enemy bullets rained through the air around him, biting at his heels, thudding into the ground. He felt a sharp tug on his right shoulder and was instantly running eight pounds lighter as the sling holding the Barnett crossbow took a direct hit and was severed, dropping the Commando on the battlefield to his rear. His right eye squinted as he ran for the helicopter, Elizabeth two paces ahead, his legs pumping up and down, up and down, his breath coming to his system in ragged gasps—wanting to stop, but knowing he couldn't.

Frost was fifteen yards from the nearest helicopter when he saw Ling clutch suddenly at his left shoulder and go down—hit but not dead. The wounded S.A.D. agent pulled himself to his feet and staggered back into the cabin of the chopper to his right. Five yards further and the 25-round stick in O'Hara's G-11 went dry, the FBI man letting the caseless gun fall to the ground as his right fist snaked for his shoulder rig and the big S&W .44 Magnum.

"Atta boy, Mike—give 'em hell!" Frost gasped as O'Hara began delivering thunder with the booming S&W.

"Come on, Frost!" O'Hara was waving the one-eyed man in with his left hand, one-handing the Model 29 with his right.

Frost stumbled, starting to fall, regaining his balance and then flying past O'Hara, his legs melting to putty, pumping up and down, up and down, his muscles working—fighting to keep him going. And then he was home, at the chopper in back of O'Hara, carrying Thoresen to the open cabin door, looking in, nodding to Ling and managing to smile, twisting left, easing Thoresen off his shoulder—Elizabeth helping—both of them offering the unconscious American to the arms of medics inside the machine.

Frost turned and faced Elizabeth. "We made it, kid."

"I always knew we . . ." she began—and then there was a shot, rising above the others. Elizabeth froze in mid-sentence, opening her mouth to scream but no sound coming out, the left side of her uniform soaking wet with blood. "Hank," she somehow got out, falling into his arms. Frost supporting her, his right eye flashing to the side and locking on the woman's assassin—a stocky Chinese terrorist wearing knee-high leather boots and a jumpsuit of khaki brown.

The one-eyed man lifted Elizabeth, holding her wounded body out to the medics in the helicopter, feeling their hands taking her weight from his, then watching as she was lowered onto a gurney secured to the cabin floor.

"It does not seem fair, Hank." The woman's words were weak. "To have come so far, to have made it to the . . ."

"Shhhh." Frost caressed her forehead.

"I will miss you, Hank Frost."

"Shhh," he told her, "you're gonna be okay. And to prove it to you, I'll make you a promise—the next time you and I go for a walk late at night—you drop that blanket. Deal?"

The helicopter's rotor blades were beginning to turn as Elizabeth reached out to lightly touch her fingertips to Frost's face. "It is a deal."

Her hand fell back to the gurney and Frost turned away from the helicopter. Elizabeth—he had seen death too often to mistake it.

"Bastard!" he screamed at the fleeing image of the terrorist who had killed Elizabeth, pushing his way past O'Hara, and racing after the killer.

"Frost!" O'Hara shouted, trying to stop him, but the

one-eyed man was beyond it.

Frost tore across the field with a vengeance, running after Elizabeth's killer, determined to bring the man down. His legs screamed—he didn't listen. Nothing would keep him from it.

A fat female terrorist attacked from the left, getting less than ten feet of her obese body before Frost, functioning on automatic now, reflexively wheeled toward the woman, bowling her over with four 9mm JHPs from the KG-99, then continued running. Next came a Night Ghost—leaping at the one-eyed man, wielding a pair of chan-mah-tao butterfly knives. Frost dispatched the black-clad figure in mid-air—almost as an afterthought—the KG-99 bucking in his hands.

Frost rounded the corner of the infirmary building and he heard—not feeling any more—mad laughter break from his lips. The terrorist who had murdered Elizabeth had decided to stop running and confront his pursuer. The killer's Type 56 assault rifle was already lining up on Frost's chest when the one-eyed man dropped belly-flat to the ground, rolled hard to the left, returning to an upright position with his KG-99 spitting death.

The assassin had time to trigger off a single shot from his rifle, the round burrowing harmlessly into the earth beside Frost's knee before Frost emptied the KG-99's magazine into his target's body. The killer was crashing to the dirt when O'Hara came charging up.

"Frost, you're crazy!"

"I got him, Mike. I got the bastard that killed Elizabeth."

"Good—we'll talk about it up in the air. The chopper and Ling and Thoresen aboard already lifted off. They're holdin' the second one for us. Come on."

"She would have done the same for me . . ."

166

Chapter Twenty-two

There was a knock at the front door, but Frost wasn't in the mood to get up and answer it.

"It's unlocked," he called out.

The knob turned, the door opened, and a half-minute later O'Hara was sitting across from Frost—pouring them both a glass of scotch from a bottle whose label depicted a Chinese elder with a long white beard, wearing a kilt and playing bagpipes.

"Ugghh," O'Hara made a face as he tasted his drink. "This tastes like paint thinner."

"I've never tasted paint thinner," Frost observed, taking a swallow of his drink.

O'Hara kept talking. "It's better to drink this stuff straight. For all we know, the crap in the local water supply could do us in. The alcohol content of this stuff would probably kill just about any bugs you can name, but you can't be too careful." He raised his glass. "Cheers."

"What are we drinking to?"

O'Hara shrugged. "Does it matter?"

"No."

"Good—then we're drinking to get drunk."

"I'm for that," the one-eyed man admitted, taking another drink. "This is terrible. How come you didn't get any of your Myers's dark rum?"

"They didn't have any—dark, light or in-between. I was lucky to get this. Bonnie-Boy Scotch," he read from the label, "The Pride of the Highlands."

"The 'Highlands' of Nanking, you mean." Frost picked the bottle up for a look. "This stuff is brewed here in town. Nothing's sacred any more."

Frost took another daring sip at his drink and settled back into the stiff-backed piece of furniture disguised as a chair, trying to get comfortable. For the most part, he realized, the commando raid to save Bruce Thoresen had been a success. Thoresen had been rescued before his abductors could kill him, and was now resting quietly in a guarded hospital room in Nanking, five miles from the hotel O'Hara and he were staying in.

Preliminary medical reports showed that Thoresen's kidnappers had both drugged and tortured the American. The mental and physical strain on the man had been tremendous, with his initial treatment by physicians being as much for shock as for anything else. Since entering the hospital the previous night, Thoresen's moments of consciousness had been sporadic at best, usually lasting no more than two or three minutes before the man went under again. It was during one of those periods, though, at 4:30 in the morning, that Thoresen had revealed the truth. While it was true Frost and the others had saved his life, they had done so after the emissary had performed for the pro-Soviet terrorists in a staged video taping of Yankee imperialist dog confessing his horrible crimes.

Frost took another drink, deciding that the paint-thinner-tasting scotch wasn't so bad after all. "If we don't hear from Ling before six," he turned his glass so the liquor swirled inside, "then I'm gonna have room service send up another bottle."

"Now, you're talkin'." O'Hara's blue eyes lit up. "An' while they're at it, they can send up some hamburgers and a couple orders of fries, too."

"I thought you liked Chinese food."

"So did I, but nobody here seems to know how to cook it. If ya ask me, they oughtta send over to the States for some recipes. You sure as hell won't find any cobra-stew on the menus back home." He looked at his watch. "What time did old Ling say he was gonna check in with us?"

"It all depends on how fast his S.A.D. guys can get one of the terrorists captured during the raid to talk."

O'Hara chuckled. "That shouldn't take too long. Ling's boys are good at that."

"Yeah." Frost closed his eye, his head beginning to feel the effects of his drink, thinking once more to himself about the assault on the island fortress. Although Thoresen had been rescued, the video tape of his confession was nowhere to be found. No video recorders, portable or otherwise, had turned up either—prompting Frost to believe that the tape and the equipment used to record it were gone from the fortress long before he and Elizabeth had shown up. "Damn."

"Now what?" O'Hara asked.

"I was thinking about Elizabeth."

"Oh."

"She was one hell of a woman, Mike."

"One of the best, Frost. I told ya that the first time I saw her talkin' to Ling."

"I remember."

"Yeah, then you should also remember how she was mixed up in this lousy mess because she wanted to be. Listen, Frost, I know you're torn up about her gettin' . . . well, about what happened. I'm pissed, too. But what we might be feelin' right now hasn't got anythin' to do with the reason we were originally tapped for this assignment. Sure, we managed to pull Thoresen away from the wolves, but the job's not finished."

"You mean the tape."

"Right," O'Hara said. "Part of me says the damn

tape probably burned in that fire you and Elizabeth started on the island. I think like that and then all of our troubles are over. But then a voice in the back of my head tells me to forget it. You told me you searched all the rooms on your way upstairs looking for Thoresen?''

Frost nodded. ''We ... we didn't see any video gear. Nothing. It's like I said earlier—my guess is that the tape and all the rest of the stuff was off the island before we ever arrived.''

''Yeah—I agree with ya. Havin' the tape destroyed in the fire would let us off the hook too easy. The terrorists wouldn't have let that happen. As soon as they had Thoresen's performance down on tape, they woulda gotten it the hell out of there.''

''So all we need to do is to find out where they took it,'' Frost said, finishing his drink and reaching for a cigarette, when a knock sounded on the door. ''It's unlocked.''

The door opened and in walked Ling, his left shoulder slumped, his coat bloodstained, the arm supported by a sling.

''Gentlemen,'' Ling said by way of a greeting.

''How's the shoulder, Ling?'' Frost asked.

''Fine, thank you.''

O'Hara held up the bottle of scotch. ''Join us in a drink?''

''Bonnie-Boy Scotch,'' Ling read the label. ''You're braver than I thought, Mike.''

O'Hara laughed. ''I take it you don't want any then?''

''Only because I'm on medication,'' the S.A.D. operative admitted.

Frost got a Camel going with the Zippo lighter, then said to Ling, ''Well, how'd those guys of yours do? They come up with anything we can use?''

Ling pulled up a chair and sat down. ''Yes. Normally, our tutors enjoy a certain degree of flexibility. Most of

170

them prefer taking their time with a subject. Under the present circumstances, however, such freedom had to be eliminated. We needed answers quickly, so our tutors saw to it that the answers were given quickly."

"Uh-huh." Frost inhaled, then exhaled the smoke from his cigarette. "And what about the tape?"

"As you suspected, Captain Frost—the tape was removed from the island shortly after Mr. Thoresen's confession was recorded. If the information our tutors acquired is correct—the tape is on its way out of China even as we speak."

"Well, if you know all that," O'Hara practically shouted, "then why the hell aren't ya chasin' it down?"

"It's not that simple. We know the tape is being taken out of China, but we are uncertain of the exact route being used."

"Then how does that help us?" O'Hara grumbled.

"We do not know how the tape will be smuggled out of China," Ling replied, "but we do know where the tape will be given over to the Russians."

"And where's that?" Frost asked.

"Nepal," Ling answered. "The tape will be taken to a remote village some distance from Khatmandu, given to the Russians, and then be flown to the Soviet Union."

"We've got to intercept the transfer, then," Frost concluded. "Any chance of flying us to Khatmandu?"

"Of course. The Mayo-Gwantsi will be ready to depart within the hour."

"I'm sorry I asked," Frost told him. "This transfer in Nepal—I suppose that's out of your jurisdiction? Something like that?"

"Correct. You and Agent O'Hara will have to go alone—and without diplomatic sanction."

"Who cares?" O'Hara downed the last of his drink, then smiled to Frost. "See, buddy? This is the break we were lookin' for. Believe me, Frost, when we hit Khatmandu and get up to that village you're gonna feel a whole lot better about all of this. You know what I mean?"

"Yeah," Frost nodded. He didn't think O'Hara knew what O'Hara meant either.

Chapter Twenty-three

"One-thousand-four, one-thousand-five, one-thousand-six . . ."

"Will you stop counting, O'Hara?"

"But I'm almost finished."

"So am I. Your counting the bricks on the walls like that is driving me nuts. I don't know why you're doing it anyway. You've already counted them twice."

"Sure, but each time I got a different answer. One-thousand-seven, one-thousand-eight . . ."

Frost filtered out the monotonous drone of O'Hara's voice, concentrating on matters at hand. Their arrival in Khatmandu, with the exception of the confusion they encountered at the city's Tribhuvan Airport, had progressed smoothly. Frost and O'Hara had waved farewell to the Mayo-Gwantsi's intrepid flight crew, processed through customs, and were soon out of the airport and on their way to the American Embassy where their weapons had been delivered ahead of them.

"I'm not going to ask why you need all of these," the Ambassador had confided as he turned the weapons over. "Washington didn't see fit to inform me, so I'll let it go at that. It's none of my business. I will say this, though, whatever you've got cooking be damn careful it doesn't boil over into your laps. If that should happen, you're on your own. There's not a thing I, or anyone associated with the Embassy, can do to help you."

They had thanked the Ambassador for his advice,

then hired a car to take them eastward over the rim of Khatmandu valley, on the buff-colored highway leading to the city of Kodari, near the Chinese border. From Kodari, they employed a guide and horses to take them further into the mountains, and to the village where Thoresen's video-taped confession was to be turned over to the Soviets.

Following the winding mountain trails they had reached their destination after a six hour ride, securing lodgings in one of the village's two-story mud and brick houses, then settling down to await word from their Nepalese contact as to when the transfer of the incriminating video tape was to be made.

And so they had waited for the past two days—cooped up together and away from the blizzard-like conditions outside—biding their time until they were given the word the transfer was on. The last piece of information their Nepalese contact had supplied was that three Russians had taken up lodgings in a house at the opposite end of the village during the middle of the previous night.

Frost stopped dwelling on the time they had wasted waiting for something to happen, and glanced over to O'Hara who was wearing a sour expression.

"What's the problem?" Frost asked. "How come you're not counting?"

"I finished."

"Thank goodness for that. Why the long face then?"

"The total I got was different from my other two counts."

"So, just take the average of the three and you should have a pretty fair idea of how many bricks we've got in our room."

"You don't think I'm countin' the bricks 'cause I'm bored, do you?"

"Nah," Frost yawned, "but if you count 'em again I can't be held responsible for my actions."

"Don't worry. I'm tired of the bricks. What do you say the two of us take a stroll to the other side of town and have a friendly chat with our neighbors from Moscow?"

"We can't, O'Hara. If we nail the Russians now the transfer won't be made, and if it isn't made, then we'll lose the chance of recovering the tape. The tape will disappear, only to resurface at a later date, and this whole trip will have been for nothing."

"Okay, okay." O'Hara threw his hands into the air. "I give up. I surrender. You've convinced me."

"To forget about visiting the Russians?"

"No," O'Hara sighed, "to start counting the bricks again. One, two, three, four . . ."

"Captain Frost! Captain Frost!"

It was three hours later and the one-eyed man was fighting to remain awake when he heard Bhim, their Nepalese contact in the village, come tramping upstairs to their room—news! Frost stood and stretched and reached for his coat—a foul-weather parka insulated with Thinsulate.

"How've you been, Bhim?" Frost greeted. "What's the good word? Is it time for us to go outside?"

"Oh, indeed it is, Frost-sahib," Bhim returned in clipped sing-song fashion. "We must go very, very immediately."

"What about the Russians?" O'Hara asked, pulling his own insulated parka over his lanky frame. "What are they up to?"

"The Communists," Bhim reported, spitting on the floor, "have already departed."

"Damn," Frost swore. "How long ago?"

"Not to be upset, Sir-sahib. The Communists," he spit again, "have left the village, but their destination is not unknown to me. There are many paths leading to where they are going. They are but taking one. I know

175

of another. It is . . . how you would call? A shortest cut."

Frost looked suspiciously to O'Hara. "Where have I heard that one before?" Then he said to Bhim, "Where are the Russians headed for, and how far away are they going?"

Bhim seemed to calculate his reply, then answered. "They are walking to a small hut very further up in the mountains. I think maybe it is three smokes from my village."

"Smokes?" O'Hara repeated. "What's that—the Nepali word for miles?"

"Oh, goodness me, no," Bhim laughed, taking out his pipe from inside his coat pocket and showing it to O'Hara. "How far I can walk in a single pipeful—that is one smoke. I would have to refill my pipe three times before I would reach the mountain hut by the path the others are taking."

"And what about this shortcut you mentioned?" Frost asked. 'How many 'smokes' will it take us to reach the hut going that way?"

"That not very easy to judge today—it pretty very freezing cold outside, but I think we make it to the hut before the second smoke is through. It very good shortest cut."

"I'm sure it is," Frost agreed, then turned to O'Hara. "Whatta ya say you and me and Bhim take a look at this shortcut of his? How's that grab ya?"

"Like we should've left ten minutes ago," O'Hara shot back. "Two smokes from now I plan to do some smokin' on my own. And you know somethin', Frost? The Russians ain't gonna like it one damn bit . . ."

The bitter wind was like an icy slap across the face as Frost and O'Hara followed Bhim through the snow-laden village, past the prayer cloths staked to hard wooden poles driven into the rock-solid earth, then along a slender trail that eventually branched off to several lesser paths to the left and right.

Although Bhim had reported that the Soviets had already started for the hut, it was impossible from simply examining the ground to determine if the Russians had crossed the trail ten minutes before. The snow was falling so heavily that any footprints made on the ground would have been completely filled in and obliterated within seconds.

Taking the smallest path, the one going to the right, Frost and the others soon left the trail they had started out on and began to climb—Frost marveling at how Bhim was able to keep the tobacco in his pipe burning in spite of the fierce wind whipping about them. Up and up they made their way, climbing along their path, moving higher into the mountains, Frost's right eye stinging and tearing from the terrible cold. No one spoke. There was no need to. All he and O'Hara had to do was remember to keep walking, forget about the freezing temperatures, and to go where Bhim led them. After that the rest was easy . . .

By Frost's Rolex, the walking time for two of Bhim's smokes was approximately ninety minutes. But Bhim's shortcut had gotten them to the site of the mountain hut well in advance of the Russians. Their Nepalese guide had shown them a sheltered area nearby where they could watch the hut unobserved, then wished the Americans good luck and told them, *"Namaste!"*—which was Nepali for both goodbye and welcome.

"Sure you don't want to stay around?" Frost had joked.

"Oh, no—Frost-sahib, I humbly submit that I cannot. I have been paid ever so wonderfully handsome to act as your contact and guide—a true honor, I assure you—but I was not paid so high as to feel so very most obligated to remain by your side while you await the Communists." He spit on the ground. *"Namaste,* gentlemen-sahibs!"

177

"Hey, hold on," O'Hara intervened. "How are we supposed to get back to your village without your help?"

"That is very easy problem to solve. If you survive what surely will be a very big fight, then you need only go back down the path as the way we came. If you do not survive, then the way from here to my village will be of no concern. You will be beyond any guidance I could give you."

"Thanks for the pep talk," Frost had said, and then Bhim had cupped his hands over the bowl of pipe and turned to walk away. A minute late he was lost from sight . . .

Frost thought to himself that Bhim was probably more than halfway home to his village by now and still—forty-five minutes after their Nepalese contact and guide had departed—there was no sign of the Russians. Frost's teeth were chattering, his eyepatch felt like it was frozen to his face, and he was ready to vote that Bhim had gotten his wires crossed and led them to the wrong mountain hut, when the one-eyed man saw them—four Russians dressed and bundled in accordance with the severity of the sub-zero weather, each wearing a Soviet AK-74 assault rifle slung over his shoulder.

As Frost and O'Hara watched, one of the Soviets broke away from the rest, moving ahead to make sure that the tiny hut was empty, then signaling to his comrades that it was safe for them to enter. One by one, the Russians walked past Frost and O'Hara's place of concealment, filed into the hut, and soon had the workings of a small fire underway inside.

"Well," O'Hara whispered, "we've got the Russians where we want 'em. Now all we're missing is the final ingredient—the Chinese terrorist delivering the video tape of Thoresen's confession. What's keeping him?"

Frost whispered in response, "I was beginning to wonder the very same thing."

Chapter Twenty-four

"I was buttering a chapati this morning and I found a hair in the butter," O'Hara said.

"Goat's hair," Frost confirmed. "That's how the Nepalese villagers make their butter—in goatskins with the skin-side turned out . . ."

"And the hair-side turned in. I know. It sort of kills my appetite."

"Then why are you talking about breakfast? That was hours ago."

"I know that, Frost. But if I don't think and talk about somethin' else besides how cold I am, I may just roll over and freeze to death."

"It is a little chilly."

"That's like callin' the middle of the Sahara in the middle of the summer a little warm. Of course it's 'chilly'—Jeez!"

"Look on the bright side, Mike. We may be stuck out in the open, but we're wearing warm clothes, we've got a windbreak protecting us, and it's stopped snowing. Put all of those pluses side-by-side next to the minor discomfort of being outside, and I think you'll have to agree with me that you're complaining about nothing."

"Bull. You don't expect me to swallow any of that crap, do you?"

Frost mumbled his reply. "Not really!"

The Russians had been waiting inside the one room brick-and-mud hut for more than an hour. From time to time one of their number would venture outside, apparently just long enough to check and see if their contact with the video tape was arriving, then quickly dart into the hut to the warmth of a pine log fire. Frost could tell it was pine they were burning from the smell of smoke spewing from the hut's tiny chimney.

Wearing fingerless wool mittens, the one-eyed man kept his hands inside the insulated pockets of his parka. Beneath his regular clothes he wore a set of thermal underwear—tops and bottoms—but even so, the continued exposure to the frigid mountain climate was beginning to numb his system, slowing his circulation, making him want to yawn. Frost realized that what he needed to do was to get moving, do some walking and exercise his legs to get his internal furnace working at capacity again. But under the present circumstances, such moving about was an impossible luxury neither he nor O'Hara could afford. Until it was time for them to attack the hut, they were restricted to staying where they were.

"Frost!" O'Hara's voice was a near-silent hiss.

"Yeah, Mike—I see him. We've got company."

As they watched from their concealed position, a long figure, dressed in a shaggy fur coat with a hood pulled over his head and shielding most of his face, gradually made his way up the trail leading to the hut. Frost removed his hands from the pockets of his parka, unzipped his coat, and quietly reached inside for the Interdynamics KG-99 taped there. With the bolt eased forward, he took one of the assault pistol's thirty-six round magazines from the cargo pocket of his parka, slapped the magazine into its well, then pulled out the operating handle from the safe position all the way to the rear, releasing it and chambering the first round.

Next to Frost, O'Hara had opened up his coat and removed the S&W Model 29 .44 Magnum he habitually

180

carried, then leaned over to Frost and said, "This is it, sport. Another coupla minutes and it'll all be over."

But instead of answering, Frost cautioned his friend to silence as the lone figure approaching from the east reached the hut's doorway, threw back his hood from his head, and stepped through the entrance.

"Son-of-a-bitch!" O'Hara exclaimed. "Did you see who that was?"

"Yeah, I saw."

"It was Ling!" O'Hara stammered, his voice reflecting a mood of hurt disbelief. "That dirty rat was sellin' us down the river all along. How could I have been so blind? Hell, I was even startin' to like the guy, and now he turns out to be a traitor."

"We don't know that for sure," Frost cautioned.

"Are you kiddin'? The Russians are here, Ling is here, and right now the Soviets are havin' the video tape of Thoresen's confession dropped into their hot little hands. What more do you want, Frost? That bastard Ling was playing us for suckers right from the start."

"I don't think so, Mike. I . . ."

The cracking sound of shots suddenly erupted from inside the hut as the door to the place burst open and three of the Russians came running out, turned rapidly to the left and hurried down the trail Ling had taken to the hut—the Russian in the lead slipping a small black plastic case into his coat as they ran.

Frost and O'Hara were on their feet and racing across the snow-covered trail for the hut as the last of the fleeing Soviets vanished over a ridge.

"They're gettin' away with the tape!" O'Hara growled.

"We gotta check on Ling first," Frost told him.

Then they were charging through the open doorway and into the hut, immediately aware of two bodies sprawled on the hut's dirt floor—one of the four

181

Russians and Ling—the Chinese agent's Type 64 silenced pistol a foot away from his outstretched hand.

"Ling!" O'Hara rushed to the man's side, cradling Ling in his arms, "What the hell happened?"

Ling licked his lips and coughed, the action sending more blood pulsing from the bullet wound in his chest. "I . . . I told you when we met in Hong Kong that the mouse does not seek cheese in the lion's mouth. Sadly, I did not heed my own advice." He coughed again, drops of blood flecking across his chin.

"Hey, Ling, take it easy." O'Hara shifted his weight, trying to make Ling more comfortable. "Everything's gonna be fine."

"I managed to intercept the courier bringing the tape to the Russians, but there was no time for me to return the tape to China. Nor could I contact you or Captain Frost without possibly alerting the Russians that we were aware of their meeting site. That . . . that's when I decided to enter the lion's mouth and take the courier's place . . . to take his place and attempt to get the Russians as well. It was . . . a tragic mistake . . ."

O'Hara's voice sounded tight, like it was ready to crack. "You didn't make a mistake, Ling. I would've followed through as the courier and tried to nail the Russians the same as you did."

"I know you would have, Mike," Ling sighed, his words losing strength and barely above a whisper. "We are very much alike—you and I—and had we met under better circumstances . . . I think we would . . . have become . . . friends . . ."

"Hey, Ling—hold on a second. Don't go yet. I had ya figured all wrong. I was wrong about ya, Ling. Do ya hear me? Do ya . . . ?"

Frost gently touched his friend on the shoulder. "He's dead, Mike. Ling's dead."

"I was so wrong about him, Frost. So damn wrong."

O'Hara's eyes were tight, gleaming.

"We've gotta stop the Russians, O'Hara. Either that or Ling and Elizabeth both died for nothing. We've gotta stop the Russians and get back the tape. It's what Ling would have wanted us to do."

O'Hara lowered Ling's body to the floor, then stood—the sadness in his voice at the loss of a friend replaced by an edge of pure hatred. "I want those bastards bad, Frost. I want 'em bad!"

"So do I, Mike. So do I."

And together they raced from the hut.

Chapter Twenty-five

Frost guessed the Russians were no more than three minutes ahead of them as he and O'Hara rushed along the slippery footpath of ice and snow, passing over the slick ridge of rock just beyond the hut, following the trail as it twisted down the far side of the mountain. The wind was blowing harder here, colder, if that were possible. And it had started snowing again—spilling great white flakes the size of silver dollars from the dark afternoon sky. Visibility on the descending trail was reduced to thirty feet at the most.

Frost rezipped his parka to ward off the frigid blasts of air and snow striking his body. His left hand was stuffed into one of his coat's insulated pockets, while his right hand, clamped to the KG-99, felt like it was frozen solid to the gun, his exposed fingers like ice cubes. Still, they were making good time; this due in part to the fact that the Russians would be, as yet, unaware that they were being chased.

The trail made a sharp curving cut to the right and, for the briefest of moments, the blizzard seemed to evaporate, and they were able to see the three retreating Russians as they rounded a second bend on the trail a quarter mile ahead. Unfortunately, the break in the storm also afforded the Russians the same privilege, because as Frost and O'Hara redoubled their efforts to cover ground, the Soviet bringing up the rear turned and pointed excitedly in their direction. The three men wheeled as one and fled out of sight around the bend.

Then the blizzard closed in on them again, obscuring everything in a curtain of wind and ice. Frost's lungs were on fire as he and O'Hara ran down the mountain. Each breath was a burning pain searing his chest. His legs and feet were carrying him on automatic, with the steep decline they were on pulling him forward, urging him to greater speeds.

Frost shifted his right eye to the side, shaking his head to clear his eyelashes of snow, watching Mike run beside him. O'Hara—the big S&W Model 29 clenched in his right fist and pumping back and forth with each new stride—was counting softly to himself each time his moving feet touched the ground.

"One, two, three, four. One, two, three, four." On and on the lanky FBI man's chant progressed as they continued their advance, approaching at a rapid pace the next bend in the trail—the one the Russians had vanished around.

They were halfway through the turn in the trail when Frost's sixth sense survival instinct made him spin sharply to the right just as one of the Russian soldiers suddenly stepped out from behind a wall of rocks, preparing to gun them down with his AK-47.

"Mike!" Frost warned, and then he was falling, dropping to the ground, rolling to the left, and coming up firing with the KG-99, two of his six shots ripping the Soviet savagely across the gut as the soldier's weapon began spitting fire.

But the soldier remained on his feet and refused to go down. Instead, seemingly ignoring the severity of his stomach wound, the Russian lowered his rifle at Frost and charged, his AK-47 hosing slugs left and right across the trail as he ran.

Frost attempted to shift away to the right, but the icy patch of ground he was on sent him slipping to his back.

He succeeded in bringing the KG-99 around for another go at his attacker, but could tell that he'd never get a shot off in time to prevent the Russian's gun from shredding him to pieces.

The thunderous crack from O'Hara's .44 Magnum tore above the fury of the storm, the single shot from the Model 29 slamming into the Russian's unprotected side, pushing him to the precipitous edge of the mountainous trail. The soldier threw his rifle over his head as he windmilled his arms in a doomed attempt to remain upright, but gravity finally claimed him and, with a frantic scream screeching from his throat, the Russian tumbled over the precipice.

"The Commie bastard didn't seem to mind gettin' shot in the gut," O'Hara snarled as he helped Frost to his feet. "Let's see him try and ignore fallin' off the mountain."

"Thanks, Mike."

O'Hara held up the Metalified and Mag-Na-Ported 29. "Sometimes it's nice to have the power of a shockwave backin' ya up, sport. Huh?"

"We'll argue about it later. Come on."

The ambush on the trail had cost them less than a minute as they continued their chase, Frost doubting that the Russians would use the same tactic twice to try slowing them down. Within a hundred yards the trail made a U-shaped turn and then gradually leveled off—leading them into a small open valley situated between the mountain they were leaving and a taller one further on.

The howling blizzard chose that point in time to sputter and die. The wind disappeared, the snow stopped falling, and somehow a needle of sunlight pierced the veil of clouds overhead, washing the valley floor with a warm yellow glow.

"Up ahead!" O'Hara pointed at the two remaining Russians, both soldiers skirting across the barren expanse of the valley close enough for Frost to see the puffs of vapor forming at the Russians' mouths as they ran. "Where do they think they're goin'? The crazy fools are runnin' straight for the Chinese border."

"I wouldn't want Tibet on it," Frost commented with a dry laugh as they pushed their way through the thigh-high drifts of snow barring their way. "Listen!"

They heard it before they saw it—the unmistakable sound of helicopter rotor blades beating against the air, coming toward them from the far end of the valley, streaking through the sky for the Russians on the ground. As the chopper flew into view, Frost recognized it from a picture as an MBB BO 105—a rigid rotor dynamo capable of extreme precision in flight.

"Damn," Frost swore, tearing through the snow even faster. "If they hop a ride on that son-of-a-bitch, we can kiss them and the video tape goodbye!"

Frost fired the KG-99 as he ran, hoping to keep the BO 105 at bay, but the pilot continued his approach on the Russian soldiers. The chopper pulled into position just above the soldiers as the KG-99's magazine ran dry.

Mechanically, Frost changed sticks in the assault pistol, cursing his luck and his aim for having missed his target. The BO 105 was dropping slowly to pick up the men when the one-eyed man finished reloading, seating the magazine in its well with a slap, then working the bolt and chambering a round—instantaneously opening fire again as O'Hara did the same.

One of the soldiers spun around with his AK-47, the bullets from his assault fire churning up the snow in front of Frost. The one-eyed man dove hard to the left and then punched out with a spasm of shots from the KG-99—at least one of the 9mm JHPs connecting, bringing the soldier down.

The pilot was hovering less than eight feet above the ground when the cabin door on the chopper popped open and a Russian wielding an AK-47 leaned out to offer his comrade on the ground some cover fire. Three times O'Hara's booming .44 reached out—the final shot plowing into the man in the chopper, sending the body flopping from the cabin doorway to the snow-laden valley below.

Frost was running, almost to the last soldier on the ground when the Russian's hand flashed from inside his coat and brought out the case containing the video tape. Before Frost could prevent it the Russian turned and tossed the tape through the chopper's open doorway, then tried swinging his AK-47 in line with Frost's chest. Frost cut the Russian down with a three-shot semi-auto burst from the KG-99 as the BO 105's rotors began revving higher, making the chopper climb.

Frost jumped, wrapping his hands around the helicopter's struts, feeling his stomach sink as the BO 105 shot up, shaking from side to side, the pilot fighting to throw him loose—the one-eyed man hanging on, getting one arm through the cabin doorway, pulling himself up and in, his right eye fixing on the video tape, grabbing it, forcing it into his pocket, seeing the pilot swivel in his seat with a revolver in his hand. Frost turned to the left, reaching for the KG-99 on its sling, finding the gun, bringing it up, firing point-blank into the pilot's shoulder. The Russian fell back, slumping over the controls, and the chopper began to drop—skimming twenty feet over the valley floor. Frost leaned out, riding the struts, a mountainside looming dead ahead, letting go, kicking out, falling in a slide into a great drift of snow, sinking beneath it, twisting his ankle as a thundering explosion ripped across the valley.

The one-eyed man waited for the rumble of the blast to subside, then clawed his way free of the snowdrift and back into the freezing mountain air.

From a long way off he could hear O'Hara shouting his name.

Chapter Twenty-six

Back in Khatmandu late the following afternoon Frost placed a toll free call to Bess from a telephone inside the U.S. Embassy. With the video tape of Thoresen's confession concerning the proposed Sino-American mutual defense pact now safely under wraps, the one-eyed man was anxious to let Bess know that he would be returning to Atlanta within the next twenty-four hours—and that he missed her. Once the call was made Frost went back to his room to where O'Hara was waiting.

"Well, was Bess excited to hear your voice, Frost? Can't see why she should be, though."

"I suppose so."

"You look worried. What's up?"

"Nothing. There's been a change in plans."

"Oh?"

"Yeah." Frost lit a cigarette with the Zippo. "It looks like you'll be flying back to the States without me."

"How come? Bess finally came to her senses and told you not to fly home?"

"Ha, ha. No, when I called, Bess said that she was on her way to the airport."

"Where's she going?"

"London, O'Hara—and so am I."

"England, right? But I thought she was all finished with that assignment?"

"She is, but the people at INB Telecommunications got caught short and called her back to temporarily fill

189

in for a guy."

"Yeah?"

"The guy who replaced her after she left. He had an accident."

"What, broke his leg or somethin'?"

"Worse than that. He got himself killed. Bess says it was a hit and run. Something funny about it maybe."

"That settles it then, sport. I'm comin' with ya."

"Hey, hold on. There's no need for both of us to go to London."

"I know that, but I'll tag along anyway. I got some R&R comin' to me, so it may as well be in England. Besides, I could use the rest. We both could."

"Yeah," Frost nodded, then added. "We made a coupla good friends, though, didn't we, O'Hara?"

"Yeah," and the grin washed away from O'Hara's face. "Yeah—yeah, we did."

"On the plane ride over . . . ?"

"Yeah?" O'Hara nodded, looking up.

Frost smiled. "I get the seat by the window."